Sprin

D1045034

꧁ Sam sprinted across the narrow chute, over one more fence, and slid down the wall into the arena.

The Phantom saw her at once. Sam heard gasps from the grandstands, and shouts summoning help, but she watched her horse. He galloped, head swinging from side to side, then lowered in a snaking, herding motion.

Sam's world shrank to just this moment, just this horse. Everything depended on her skill at understanding him.

The stallion's forelegs braced apart and his head hung. He staggered forward a step.

"Zanzibar, boy, what have they done to you?" ꧂

Phantom Stallion

◦◦ 4 ◦◦
The Renegade

TERRI FARLEY

AVON BOOKS

An Imprint of HarperCollins*Publishers*

Library of Congress Catalog Card Number:
2002091784
ISBN 0-06-441088-9

First Avon edition, 2003

❖

AVON TRADEMARK REG. U.S. PAT. OFF. AND IN OTHER COUNTRIES,
MARCA REGISTRADA, HECHO EN U.S.A.

Visit us on the World Wide Web!
www.harperchildrens.com

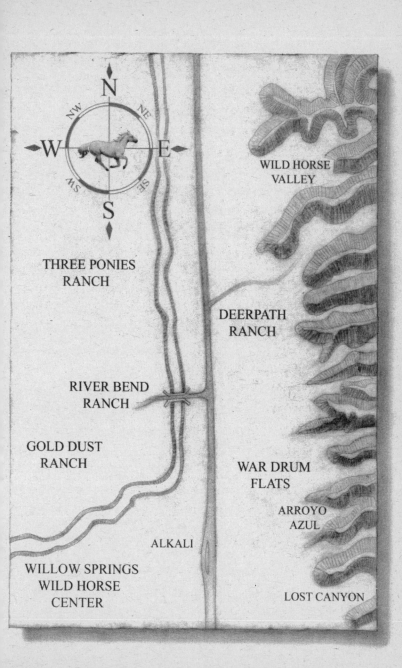

4

The Renegade

Chapter One ∽

$\mathcal{I}$n River Bend's big pasture, the horses waited for rain. Cottonwood branches danced overhead, but instead of rustling, the dry leaves clacked. The horses stood with heads up and nostrils wide, searching for a trace of moisture on the breeze.

Across the dirt driveway, near the house, Sam did the same. She stood in the vegetable garden, where she was supposed to be turning over dirt to mix parched cornstalks and empty vines with the earth. Instead, she leaned on her shovel and wished she'd brought a water bottle outside with her.

Two sparrows dove for a worm her digging had uncovered. The birds cheeped and quarreled, then flew off in a flurry of feathers, leaving the lucky worm untouched.

Sam looked skyward. The noon sun was sealed down by a lid of gray clouds.

Irritated whinnies and the thud of hooves came

from the big pasture. Banjo, Dad's roping horse, bolted across the sparse grass. Teeth bared, Strawberry sprinted after him.

Except for a few hammering rainstorms that ran off the drought-hardened land, it hadn't rained since spring. Now it was October. Every creature was edgy with waiting.

More hooves thudded inside the round pen, but these made a soothing sound, just like the voice that directed them.

"Other way," Jake said. "Good horse."

Friday after school, Jake had mounted Teddy Bear for the first time. Now it was Saturday morning, and the colt was already responding to the bit and reins.

The morning quiet didn't last for long. Blaze burst barking from the barn, and Sam noticed a plume of dust approaching the ranch. The roar of an overtaxed engine told her who was driving even before the beige Cadillac crossed the bridge too fast and skidded into the ranch yard.

Sam dropped the shovel. For their neighbor Linc Slocum, everything was a crisis. Still, it was always possible it was a real emergency.

The Cadillac's horn blared, even though Gram had already appeared, wiping her hands on her apron. Dallas, the ranch foreman, had emerged from the shady barn, blinking against the sunlight.

Jake slipped out of the round corral and beat everyone to Slocum's side.

"Rachel's missing," Linc said as Sam got close enough to hear.

Gram patted Linc's arm as the man removed his oversized cowboy hat and sighed.

"I don't know what to think," he explained. "I'd just got back from riding with Jed." Linc scanned faces, making sure they recognized the name of Jed Kenworthy, his foreman. "But he stayed out with the other hands and I came back. Otherwise I sure would've got him helping me."

"How long has she been gone?" Gram asked.

"Hard to say. Let's see." Linc squinted as he tried to recall. "When I got back home, Rachel was lazing around her suite and then I had a snack and after that I sorta dozed off." He shook his head. "I'd say at least a coupla hours."

Sam's eyes slid toward Jake. Jake was only sixteen, but he spotted trouble better than anyone Sam knew. And he didn't look worried. In fact, when he crossed his arms over his belt buckle, he seemed to be telling Linc to get to the point.

"Thing is," Slocum said, sounding as if he were about to make a confession, "she was perturbed about something. In fact, she's been sort of put out—say, how long has it been since I had the rodeo stock contractor over to the house?" Slocum mused a minute. "All week. Yessir." Linc sounded amazed. "She's been perturbed all week long."

For an instant, Sam wondered how he could tell

perturbation from Rachel's usual attitude, but then she understood his amazement. How could Rachel be dissatisfied for a full week? She wore the finest clothes and makeup. A driver took her to school in a baby blue Mercedes Benz, and her bedroom suite included a hot tub and state-of-the-art entertainment systems.

Rachel was her father's princess, and she pretty much ruled Darton High School, as well. Her face, hair, and figure might have been composed by a computer designing the perfect girl.

Too bad no one had pushed the button marked "personality," Sam thought.

"Could the stock contractor have said something to upset her?" Gram asked.

"No, no way." Linc actually blushed. "We were cutting a deal for my Brahmas, that's all."

Did Linc redden because the stock contractor had rejected his bulls? City-bred Slocum really didn't know what he was doing when it came to animals, Sam thought. He just liked playing cowboy.

"Where do you think she's got off to?" Dallas asked. He sounded more sympathetic than Sam felt.

"Did she take a car?" Jake added. Though Rachel didn't have a driver's license, she wouldn't let such a formality stop her.

"No, she didn't, and no one came to pick her up or I would've heard tires." Linc wedged a thumb into the tooled leather belt that strained around his middle. "But my horse is missing, to

"Why would she take Champ? horses," Sam blurted.

"Well now—" Slocum frowned.

"She does," Sam insisted. "She says they're dumb and dirty, and she can't understand why anyone likes them."

Gram made a cautioning sound, but Sam knew she was right.

"I don't mean to be rude, Mr. Slocum, but she told me all that herself."

"My ex-wife made the twins ride for three hours every day when they were little," Slocum said. "Ryan took to it and Rachel didn't. Maybe that's why he's in England. Now that his mom's married that baron, or whatever he is, they have stables packed with horses."

Slocum sounded wistful. For about two seconds, Sam felt sorry for him. Then she remembered the spade bit he used on Champ, his gentle-natured palomino. In the hands of an excellent rider, the bit could work. Hauled on by an angry girl who didn't like horses, that bit could do terrible damage to Champ's tender mouth.

"Let's go find her," Sam said.

"I'll be glad to pay—" Slocum began.

"Land sakes, Linc, will you hush?" Gram snapped. One of her hands darted out as if she wanted to give Slocum a pinch. Instead, she shook her finger at him. "We'll help because we're neighbors, not because you have money."

Gram took Western neighborliness seriously. Her tirade made Linc look sheepish.

"Wyatt's checking the herd with Ross and Pepper," Gram said, "but the rest of us will saddle up. I don't imagine she's gone far. Have you called over to the Elys'?"

Gram gestured toward the Three Ponies Ranch, Jake's home.

"No," Linc said. "I think Rachel would be embarrassed. Mainly I came for Jake."

Jake shrugged modestly. Sam wished she had a skill she could be humble about. Jake was a first-rate tracker. Local ranchers, the Bureau of Land Management, and even the sheriff's department knew it.

"Sure," Jake said. His eyes darted skyward at a rumble of far-off thunder. "I'd want to start at your ranch, though."

"You do that," Gram said. "And, Linc, we'll go up the ridge trail, since it runs behind your place, ours, and Three Ponies." Gram removed her apron and started for the barn and her mare, Sweetheart.

"Hop in, Jake." Slocum gestured toward the Cadillac, but Jake glanced at the round corral, where Teddy Bear stood saddled and curious.

"I'll take care of the colt," Dallas said. "You go on."

Sam bit her lip. Jake had teased her forever, calling her a tagalong brat, but she couldn't help it. "I'd really like to watch you track," she said.

Jake didn't reply. Did he suspect she also wanted to see Rachel uncomfortable?

Sam stared hard at the back of Jake's head as he unstrapped the short, fringed chaps called chinks and slung them over the top rail of the corral.

Finally, her brain waves must have penetrated his thick skull.

"You might as well come." He didn't even look her way. "Rachel might not be so embarrassed with you there."

He was right, Sam thought as she climbed into the Cadillac's backseat. She brought out Rachel's natural snobbishness. Rachel couldn't believe there were people who actually liked "the little cowgirl," as she called Sam.

Sam tightened her seat belt, as Linc Slocum drove fast and recklessly. If he was so worried, why hadn't he gone looking for Rachel himself?

Jake grabbed an armrest as Slocum swerved around a turn. Sam hoped Linc wouldn't hit anything. She'd hate to miss a chance to see Rachel in trouble. After the mean things Rachel had said and done, it would be sort of satisfying to see her squirm.

But that wasn't going to happen. Rachel wouldn't be punished for causing Linc to worry, and Sam knew why. When they found Rachel, she wouldn't be sunburned or dusty. Every hair would be in place and she'd blame someone else for her troubles.

When they reached Slocum's Gold Dust Ranch,

he surprised them by saying he wouldn't come along.

"I'll stay by the phone," he said. "You just take any horses you want. The tack shed's over there."

Any other time, Sam would have rejoiced. The Gold Dust Ranch was home to dozens of expensive and beautiful horses. But Jake was in a hurry. He flashed her a look that said she'd better not knock on the door to the foreman's house and tell her best friend, Jen Kenworthy, what was happening.

Sam and Jake took the mounts easiest to catch, rode past Linc Slocum's pillared mansion and up the ridge trail.

The mare Sam rode was a sturdy paint with a scar on one knee. Jake's horse was a bay Thoroughbred she'd seen Slocum ride only once before.

Jake rode automatically, attention directed toward the dirt as if he could read it like a book.

"Tell me how you do it," Sam urged after about ten minutes.

"Noon's the hardest time to track," Jake said as they rode side by side. "With the sun directly over-head, tracks just disappear. See how there are no shadows in the hoofprints?"

Jake didn't slow his horse as he pointed. Sam looked down. The ground looked bare as concrete. Except for a few drought cracks, she saw nothing.

"What hoofprints?"

Jake smiled. "Never mind. We don't have to look for clues, just a horse."

Sam didn't like Jake's superior smile any more than she liked the sweat trickling down the back of her neck.

"Don't tell me 'never mind,'" she insisted. "Tell me what to do, so when I have to come looking for *you*, it won't take so long."

This time Jake laughed aloud. "Dreamer."

Sam glared at him, but Jake wasn't looking. He told her how to judge the age of a print and the weight or speed with which it had been made, but then he went back to reading the earth, as if she'd interrupted him while he was reading a good book.

They rode in silence for a while and Sam welcomed it. She hadn't seen the Phantom for weeks, but at least she could daydream about him.

Everything reminded her of the great silver stallion. The rocks and ridges around her seemed painted with his shadow. When she heard the rasp of a tool from Slocum's ranch down below, it sounded like the Phantom's neigh of surprise.

As the trail twisted around the mountain, rising higher, Sam looked down on River Bend Ranch and the silver-brown glitter of the river. The stallion's vast territory spread from here to the Calico Mountains. She looked east, past War Drum Flats. That wisp of white on the mountain was probably a thin curl of cloud, but it could be the Phantom's windblown mane and tail.

Jake must have taken her silence for pouting,

because he reined in the Thoroughbred and started an exasperated lecture, as if she'd been silently begging him to do it.

"Okay, if Rachel had been lost overnight," Jake said, "there'd be more of us in the search party. We'd form groups, divide up the area, and check each section on foot. Or maybe we'd use airplanes and ATVs. We'd check every little splinter road . . ."

Jake's voice trailed off as something drew his attention away from the trail and down the hillside toward a clump of brush.

"What?" Sam asked.

"Nothing. And since the horse—and not Rachel—is probably in charge, he'll stick to the path, where the footing is easy. Here, look at this." Jake reined his horse back the way they'd come and dismounted.

He walked along, pointing. "See, the hoofprints are pretty close together and pretty distinct, then there's this big mishmash of tracks."

Sam climbed off the paint, squatted next to Jake, and stared. Finally she saw horseshoe prints, one on top of the other. "Yeah," she said.

"Something scared Champ. I'm thinking maybe deer, down in that brush. Rachel probably wouldn't think of trying to pet him and calm him down. So he stayed scared, she couldn't handle him, and look—" Jake pointed to widespread hoofprints. "He's running, kind of off balance, and pretty soon we'll see where she fell."

"How can you be so sure? Linc said she had riding lessons."

"Well, she's forgotten what she learned." Jake's finger moved through the air. "Champ's veering left, right, all over the place. She's jerking him around. Pretty soon he'll get sick of it, or the bit will hurt enough that he'll decide the deal is off."

With horses, it was all about trust. That's what Sam had been taught since she was old enough to listen. Dad said horses were big, strong animals who agreed to do what you wanted them to do as long as you knew what you were doing.

Rachel clearly wasn't doing her part.

Suddenly, Sam could see where Champ had balked. Four hoofprints were planted in a square, as if someone had used a kitchen table like a stamp.

"Bet she went over his head," Jake muttered as they remounted.

They'd only ridden a few minutes when the trail split. Jake chose the path that slanted down and left. They'd only ridden a few yards when Rachel's voice, distinctive because of its faint English accent, soared toward them.

"Get away from me, horse. *Away*, I said, or you'll be sorry."

Jake gave Sam a smug look, congratulating himself on picking the right path, just as Rachel stormed into view.

Her coffee-colored hair lay in a shiny wing across

her forehead. She wore a red silk blouse and tan boots that looked soft as the nose of the palomino following her.

But Rachel's designer jeans were ripped to show bloody knees, and the palm pushing her hair back looked raw, as if she'd used her hands to break her fall.

"Rachel, are you okay?" Sam asked.

Rachel stopped. Champ halted behind her, though his bobbing head said he wanted to touch noses with the other horses.

"Aren't you rather far from your 'spread'?" Rachel's lips twisted as if Sam and Jake were viruses that had escaped from a lab.

She didn't seem happy to be rescued. Jake darted a glance at Sam. She didn't think he was surprised by Rachel's ingratitude. Then he frowned past Sam, toward the mountains.

Maybe if Rachel understood the worry she'd caused, she'd be nicer.

"Your dad was afraid you were lost, so we came looking for you," Sam explained. "My grandmother and Dallas are searching, too."

"Clearly, I am not lost." Rachel understood, all right. She just didn't care.

"Sorry for interrupting your walk," Sam said, pretending to turn the paint mare back toward the Gold Dust Ranch.

"I'm not lost," Rachel said loudly, "but I am frustrated with this horse. He wouldn't let me remount after I, um, climbed down to admire the view."

The only view Rachel had been admiring was one of the earth rushing up to meet her hands and knees, but Sam didn't say so.

Rachel stumbled forward as Champ nuzzled her backbone. The horse wasn't holding a grudge, but Rachel was. She whirled around to scold him just as Jake leaned toward Sam and whispered, "Don't look behind you."

When they were little, Sam had told Jake he had "mustang eyes." Sometimes the label still fit. Dark brown, half-wild, and hypnotic, his eyes managed to hold hers now, but barely.

Behind Sam, the trail dropped off to a steep hillside. What was there? She hadn't heard the whir of a rattlesnake, but it could be a cougar or a bear. Sam felt an almost irresistible pull to do the opposite of what Jake ordered.

"I'm going to do something loud and obnoxious." Jake barely moved his lips. "Then you can look. Got it?"

Sam nodded, but it was Rachel who spoke first.

"It's hardly polite, talking about me in whispers." Rachel faced them with one eyebrow arched.

"Not going to be using that horse anymore? Is that what you said?" Jake asked.

Rachel looked a little sickly. "If you could just hold him while I get back up—"

"No need," Jake said. He forced his horse forward,

made a loud coyote yip, and slapped his hat on Champ's hindquarters.

The palomino bolted past, headed toward home, away from Rachel's squeal of outrage.

And that's when Sam looked.

Hidden up to his shoulder in a thicket of sagebrush, the Phantom was watching them. His perfect Arab ears were pricked to catch Sam's voice, but his intelligent eyes surveyed the scene and judged it too risky for approach.

Still, he didn't flee. Instead, the stallion tossed his thick white mane in greeting, and his eyes were set on Sam.

Chapter Two ꙮ

*J*ake had probably wanted his whooping shout and Rachel's running horse to make the Phantom stampede back the way he'd come from. But he didn't.

At first, Sam admired the stallion's intelligence. The mustang knew he wasn't in danger.

Then, she felt a warning chill. He shouldn't be so trusting. There was no telling what Rachel would do. And Jake had sworn he'd never give the stallion another chance to hurt Sam.

The Phantom should never trust a human. Ever.

Once before, the Phantom's love for her had been responsible for his capture. She couldn't let that happen again.

"Now what?" Rachel demanded.

Sam wrenched her eyes away from the stallion and looked at Rachel. Hands on hips, the rich girl stared up at the riders.

"I found her," Jake said. "So you deal with her."

"Like I couldn't have just ridden along this trail and blundered into her?" Sam asked.

Hoping Rachel was distracted by their bickering, Sam dared a quick glance at the Phantom. He sidestepped off a few feet, eyes rolling white at her sharp tone.

"No, you couldn't have found her. Not without a bloodhound," Jake said. "Or me."

"Hello?" Rachel snapped her fingers. "Ex-*cuse* me? Will one of you dismount so I can ride home?"

"No," Sam and Jake said in unison.

At least they could agree on that.

"Then how do you expect to take the credit for 'saving' me?"

Rachel had a point, but Sam didn't tell her so.

"You'll have to ride double with one of us." Jake's voice cut off Rachel's whining.

Saddle leather creaked and a blue jay squawked, laughing at their predicament.

"No way," Rachel said. "Samantha, just get down and give me that horse. She belongs to me, after all, and if you can ride her, so can I."

"I'm not the one who ended up on the ground."

"You stupid girl." Rachel's eyes narrowed. "I could tell you something you'd pay your whole pitiful allowance to hear."

Like fashion advice? Or Queen Rachel's tips on snagging the popular crowd's adoration? Sam kept her lips closed and wished Gram hadn't handicapped her with good manners.

"Both of you hush up," Jake said.

"What did *I* say?" Sam cried.

Jake kicked loose from his left stirrup and pointed.

"Rachel, put your foot in there, swing up behind me, and hang on."

The bay shied at Rachel's approach and she hesitated.

"Do it now." Jake calmed the horse with a pat. "If I don't get my work done before sundown, I don't get paid."

The instant Rachel followed Jake's instructions, he set the Thoroughbred loping away.

Like something from a movie, Rachel's glossy hair swung from side to side.

As her accented voice floated back to Sam, it was clear Rachel was mulling over what Jake had said.

"That hardly seems fair." Rachel seemed puzzled by the idea of doing a fair day's work for wages.

Jake laughed. Sam tried to join him, but failed.

She could disregard Jake's amusement and ignore the fact that he'd asked Rachel to climb up behind him. What Sam couldn't overlook was the way Rachel Slocum had her arms wrapped around Jake's waist. She was doing a lot more than just holding on for balance.

Sam was so hot with jealousy, she forgot to look back for the Phantom. When she finally remembered, he was gone.

❄ ❄ ❄

When they rode into the Gold Dust ranch yard, Sam expected to see Linc Slocum waiting for his daughter. After all, Champ had run on ahead, and a saddled but riderless horse was rarely good news.

Champ had taken the right path home, but he was sweating and still saddled. Bloody foam clung to the corners of his lips, but he looked happy as he stretched over a fence to touch noses with a huge Brahma bull.

All three of them had dismounted and Jake had begun unsaddling the tired palomino when Slocum finally appeared, tucking a cell phone into his pocket.

"Soon as I saw you coming, I phoned River Bend to call off the search," Slocum said.

"Thanks," Sam said.

"Wyatt had just come in and was wondering where everyone was." Slocum gave a strained chuckle.

He looked even more out of place than usual in a pale green shirt and matching pants. Without his cowboy hat and boots, he looked a lot like a golfer.

Sam tugged at the paint mare's cinch while peeking over her back. Linc Slocum was approaching Rachel, and Sam couldn't help being nosy.

"What were you thinking, honey, to go riding off without telling me?" he asked.

Maybe his daughter's ripped jeans and the fear that she'd been hurt explained why he sounded like he was apologizing.

Rachel squared her shoulders and looked down her nose as if addressing the lowliest freshman.

"I don't want to discuss it," she snapped, then walked right past her father.

As Sam pulled the saddle off the paint's back, she listened for Linc to call Rachel back and scold her.

"Rachel, honey, I wish you'd tell me what has you so perturbed," he said.

"Later." Rachel kept walking.

Sam was amazed, but she just balanced the saddle blanket atop the heavy Western saddle, slung the bridle over her shoulder, and walked to the tack room.

The tack room smelled of fresh-cut pine boards, tended leather, and buckle polish. Sam would bet it was the result of Jed Kenworthy's work, not Slocum's.

"Nothing happened to her when she sassed her father." Sam couldn't help sharing her surprise when Jake came through the door with tack from Champ and the Thoroughbred.

"Uh-huh."

"She just walked off." Sam followed Jake. "And he didn't say anything."

"Yep." Jake hung the bridles on spindles.

"She could have ruined that horse. Don't you think I should tell him so?"

"Suit yourself," Jake said, but now he was looking at a shelf of horse medicine.

When he unscrewed the lid on a tin of salve and sniffed it, Sam wondered if Jake was just stalling to make her mad.

"You're too chicken to do it, right?" she teased.

Nothing. "Or maybe you like her."

Instead of rising to the bait, Jake glanced in a mirror on the tack room wall and adjusted the angle of his Stetson.

She'd been joking, but Jake never looked in the mirror, never took pains with his appearance. He showered, and that was it. What if Jake really *did* like Rachel? At school, dozens of guys flocked around her. They walked her to class, brought her sodas, and shared their homework.

Sam replayed the image of Jake riding double with Rachel. *Oh please, not Jake, too.*

When they came out of the tack room, Slocum was standing near the big Brahma as if he was waiting for them. Slocum should have at least offered to help with the horses, but he hadn't. He hadn't said "Thank you," either.

Filled with irritation, Sam walked right up to him.

"Mr. Slocum, Rachel could have hurt herself and Champ, riding off the way she did."

"I know." Slocum tried to hang his thumbs in his pockets as Jake did, but they wouldn't quite fit.

Sam waited. Gram would say she'd already been impolite. "Guess I'll just hope she doesn't," Slocum continued. "She never has before."

Sam bit her lower lip to keep her mouth closed.

She couldn't say another sassy word. Slocum might be smiling, but he was angry. If he talked to Gram or Dad, she was already dead.

"I'll have to be sure someone's around to unsaddle horses, so she'll leave them be." Slocum seemed to be talking to himself. "Or maybe take her mind off horses altogether, and buy her that red Porsche she's been wanting."

Sam couldn't believe her ears.

From the corner of her eye, Sam saw Jake shake his head as if Sam should know better than to take on another lost cause. She ignored him.

"Maybe," she suggested to Slocum, "you could talk with Rachel about—"

A sudden threat flared in Slocum's eyes. She stopped. She glanced at Jake. Of course he hadn't noticed. When Sam looked back to see what Slocum would do next, she decided she must have imagined the look. Slocum just shrugged and gave her a dopey smile.

"You're right, Samantha. I guess what I really need around here is a smart girl like you to tell everyone exactly what they should be doing."

"I'm sorry, Mr. Slocum." Sam hoped her sincerity showed. "I guess I got a little carried away, but Rachel fell, you know, and Champ's mouth is torn up."

"Jed keeps medicine for that," Slocum said.

Slocum watched Jake move close to the haltered and tied palomino. Gently, Jake dabbed on the salve he'd brought from the tack shed.

"I see Jake found that medicine. Good. And you don't go worrying, Samantha. You didn't hurt my feelings."

Sam didn't believe him. She felt like the sun had moved closer and the lid of clouds had pressed down tighter.

"In fact, my son, Ryan, is coming home soon. He'll help keep everything straight. Though he's more of a horseman, he's agreed to help with my new hobby."

Champ snorted and pulled against his tie rope as Slocum approached the pen that held the tiger-colored Brahma bull.

Glossy orange and black hair swirled with creamy white over the bull's saggy skin. A hump wobbled where his neck flowed into his back. He had such large, gentle eyes, he wouldn't have looked fierce at all if it hadn't been for his markings. Black tiger stripes made a mask around his eyes. Each side of the mask pointed back to his short, sharp horns.

"Meet Maniac," Slocum announced, "part of my new bucking Brahma program."

As Slocum gestured in fanfare, the bull wrenched his massive head away from the fence. Strings of saliva swung from his jaws, but he didn't bolt in fear. Once Maniac backed out of Slocum's reach, the big bull held his ground.

Sam swallowed hard. What was the bull doing? Most of the time, she could think like a horse. That made it easier to know when Ace or any other horse might spook. Range cattle seemed to react the same way. Horses and cattle loved the safety of the herd, and most chose to run away from danger.

But Maniac seemed different. His chocolate-colored eyes were watching for a challenge, but his drooping ears belonged on a velvety toy.

"He doesn't look too mean," Sam said.

"Not mean?" Slocum roared, making his voice loud enough to provoke the bull. "Watch this."

He waved his arms, too. The bull shook his head and pawed the earth once. Sam could read that message. It meant "Back off."

Before Slocum goaded the bull further, Jake sidled in and pulled the rope tethering Champ. The knot slipped, as intended. When he walked the skittish palomino past, Jake glared at Sam.

What? If he thought she'd purposely egged Slocum into making a fool of himself, Jake was wrong.

"Hey, you two-thousand-pound cheeseburger," Slocum shouted, "show the little lady what you got!"

Flinging his bulky body toward the fence, Slocum started to climb.

Maniac didn't warn again. He trotted two surprisingly graceful steps, feinted his horns to the left, then slammed forward into the fence.

Slocum fell. The side of the corral was still shuddering when he stood, dusted himself off, and gave a breathless laugh.

The bull stood huffing, eager for another dare.

"I guess you're right," Sam said quickly. She didn't want him to tease the bull anymore. "He's fierce."

"Darn tootin' I'm right. And I'm not the only one

who thinks so." Slocum beckoned Sam to come closer.

Struggling to be polite, she moved toward him.

"Last week, d'you know who I had out here?"

Sam shook her head.

"Karla Starr, of Starr Rodeo Productions. She's just getting started and you might not have heard of her yet, but you will." Slocum rubbed his hands together. "She's a cowgirl. Just a little bit of a thing, not much bigger than you, but tough. Oh my, yes, tough as a boot heel and ready to go up against the big boys who breed rough stock for rodeos. That's bucking bulls and horses," Slocum added, "in case you didn't know.

"Karla gets rough stock the old-fashioned way. She doesn't breed 'em on a big fancy ranch. She buys renegade horses and outlaw bulls from cowboys—and ranchers like me."

Sam could tell he liked the sound of that. Puffed up with pride, Slocum gave the words "ranchers like me" a chance to echo around the hot, silent ranch yard.

If only he knew how ignorant he sounded.

Renegade horses weren't born man-haters. Most had been ruined by careless, impatient humans. Sam wouldn't be surprised to learn it was the same with "outlaw" bulls.

Some of the old ways had died out because rodeo fans couldn't stand such cruelty. In the past, hundreds of mustangs were trapped, crowded into high-sided trucks, and driven hours across country. Once they reached a rodeo arena, the thirsty animals stampeded out of the truck, only to be roped and blindfolded while men slammed saddles on their backs.

Men were injured once in a while, but others usually twisted a mustang's tail or bit his ear—anything to paralyze the horse with fear until a cowboy was jammed into the saddle. Sam imagined the horses could only compare men's weight and spurring to a cougar attack.

Those were the "good old days" of rodeo. Slocum should be smart enough to know they'd ended for a reason.

"Karla Starr thinks Maniac and some of my other Brahmas could be rodeo celebrities." Slocum savored the syllables as they rolled off his tongue. "She's willing to give my critters a try in a late-fall rodeo in California—if I sweeten the deal a little."

Sam noticed Jake was still nearby, listening, but since he didn't ask the question, she did.

"What does that mean, 'sweeten the deal'?" Sam asked.

"Well, she was looking for light-colored bucking horses, mainly. Had her eye on the palominos, but Kenworthy won't sell."

Sam wondered where Slocum had found the nerve to even ask the Kenworthys to sell the last of their palominos. Before they went broke and sold out to Slocum, the Kenworthys had been known not only for their prime cattle but for Quarter horses with palomino coloring.

Only four of the horses remained. Two were mares, Mantilla and Silk Stockings, the skittish horse Jen called Silly. The other two were geldings. Jed Kenworthy rode Sundance in cutting competitions and Gold Champagne was the horse Slocum called Champ.

Sam was afraid to ask why Slocum hadn't sold Champ to Karla Starr, but he must have read her frown.

"I would've thrown Champ into the deal, but he just won't buck no matter what you do to him."

The words made Sam sick. So how had he convinced the stock contractor to take a chance on his untrained bulls? She had to know.

Sam thought of a fancy tea party with china cups and white gloves, and made her voice polite enough to match.

"Gosh, Mr. Slocum, so how *did* you 'sweeten the deal'?"

"We're still working out the details, but Miz Starr won't be disappointed."

There it was again. Slocum's sneaky half-smile hinted he was hiding a dark secret.

Sam tried to shake off her paranoia, but Slocum was worrying her.

"So, you'd sell Maniac?" she asked. "I thought he was going to be part of a breeding program."

"He was," Slocum agreed. "But breeding Brahmas

takes time. And, shoot, Maniac could be famous now."

"But in the future—" Sam began.

"Samantha, let me tell you a fact of life. When you have money, the future takes care of itself." Slocum gave her a pitying smile. "I could sell every Brahma I bought for the breeding program, then just get more of 'em before Ryan comes home, so we'd have some cows to play with. It's simple."

Just like buying Rachel off with a sports car so she wouldn't sneak Champ away. Just like buying Jed Kenworthy's ranch so Slocum had a place to play cowboy. Just like stripping all the old pine trees off the mountainside so he had a place to put his mansion.

"Mr. Slocum?" Jake shifted his weight toward Slocum's Cadillac.

"That's right. You'll be wanting to get back to the River Bend and that colt you're riding. Must be a lot of fun, showing a banker like Mr. Martinez what you can do."

"Most fun work there is," Jake agreed. "And college won't come cheap, so it's lucky I like it."

"College? I thought you'd be saving for a fast car," Slocum said as they climbed into his Cadillac. "When I was your age, that's all I did—race when the cops weren't watching."

Slocum's voice implied that Jake was a wimp if he wasn't longing for a hot car.

"He wants a car, too," Sam said, but Jake, sitting in front beside Slocum, stayed quiet.

As they pulled away from the Gold Dust Ranch, Sam looked back at the bare ridges behind Slocum's mansion. According to Gram, the piñon pines had been there for hundreds of years; they helped slow the snowmelt and kept the ranch from flooding.

Jen said that since Slocum had built his pretend plantation house, mud puddles and mosquitoes had marred the ranch until May.

Slocum probably didn't understand why. He wouldn't believe that he couldn't buy off nature.

As they drove past War Drum Flats, Sam looked for the Phantom.

A dozen times, near dawn and dusk, she'd seen wild horses watering at the little lake down there. Now, in the heat of the day, nothing moved.

Suddenly, Slocum's chuckle interrupted her thoughts.

"When they caught rodeo stock the old way, those range rats musta put on quite a show."

It was probably coincidence, the way Slocum narrowed his eyes toward the water hole she was watching for the Phantom. But his words made Sam uneasy, just the same.

Chapter Three ❧

Two noisy horses and a barking dog competed for Sam's attention as she climbed out of Linc Slocum's car.

"Blaze, simmer down," Dallas called from the bunkhouse porch. The border collie frisked around Sam's legs a minute, then obeyed, but no one could quiet the horses.

Dark Sunshine whinnied from the big pasture. While most of the horses crowded into the shade beneath the big cottonwood tree, the tiny buckskin trotted along the fence. Her black mane and tail billowed around her and her eyes watched Sam.

"She sounds better, doesn't she?" Sam asked Jake.

"Lots," Jake agreed. "That sound she used to make gave me the creeps."

Just weeks ago, the mare's neigh had chilled them all. Mustangs were usually silent, but abuse and neglect had made Dark Sunshine's neighs sound like screams.

Although Sunny was the wildest horse on the River Bend Ranch, she'd adopted the herd of saddle horses as her family. Only Popcorn matched her explosive energy as she ran laps around the ten-acre corral, and she always outlasted the albino, showing how much she missed the open range.

To help calm her, Sam made time every day after school to pony the mare. She trotted alongside as Sam rode Ace, happy to stretch her legs.

Dad and Dallas were pretty sure Dark Sunshine was in foal to the Phantom, so it was important that she exercise and become gradually more accustomed to people.

Everyone understood this—except Ace.

The bay gelding paced along the barn corral fence. Every so often he halted, pawed impatiently, and aimed a summoning snort toward Sam.

"If I believed in such things, I'd say that gelding of yours is psychic," Gram said as she walked toward them from turning Sweetheart into the pen with Ace. "He started fussing about five minutes before Blaze barked to tell us Linc's car was coming."

Sam smooched toward the corral. Ace stopped. He tossed his head so that his forelock flipped away from the white star on his forehead.

"Quit embarrassing him," Jake said. "No working cow pony likes to be treated like a pet."

"Shows how much you know," Sam said.

She would have gone to Ace right away if Jake

hadn't disappeared into the barn just as everyone else asked for details about the search for Rachel.

"Found her okay, I guess," said Dallas. The gray-haired foreman sat on the front step. He looked tired.

That morning, Dad had confided to Gram that Dallas's arthritis was acting up. Though Dallas would resist, Dad planned to ask him to do work that would keep him around the ranch.

Sam sat down beside him on the step. She tried not to be judgmental in telling how they'd found Rachel, but she couldn't resist adding a few sentences about the surprising treatment Rachel had received when she reached home.

Dad, Gram, and Dallas all shook their heads.

Gram said, "In rough country like this, someone needs to know where you are."

Sam agreed, for Rachel. But Gram and Dad wouldn't have to worry about her. "If there was an emergency," Sam began, "and I had to leave without—"

"No excuses," Dad said. "Not now and not when you're twenty-one. Never try a fool stunt like that."

"I'm not like Rachel."

Dad nodded, looking satisfied. He wouldn't say anything bad about a neighbor, but she could tell he didn't approve of bribing your child to make her behave.

"Good thing," Dallas said, pulling himself to his feet. "Because you've got a chore that needs doing.

Before you went tearing off after Jake, I planned for you to check the feed room for mice. That means moving everything in there."

"But Dallas, Sunny and Ace haven't been out today. They need exercise."

"That can wait. You're taking tomorrow morning to ride out with the Kenworthy girl. Isn't that right?"

"Yes, but—"

"I saw something out of the corner of my eye this morning in the tack room. We can't have rodents eating the winter feed."

"Dad," Sam appealed to her father. Instantly, she saw it had been a mistake.

"Dallas is the foreman. You know that."

"Yes, sir," Sam said, but as she trudged toward the barn, Sam couldn't help thinking everyone was happier when Dallas was out on the range, where he belonged.

One side of Ace's corral allowed him inside the barn. He trotted in just as Sam entered, and she couldn't resist giving him the hug he wanted.

Ace swung his head over the top fence rail, and Sam wrapped her arms around his sleek bay neck. Eyes closed, she let his coarse mane rub her cheek while his lips whuffled her shoulder.

"You are such a good horse. I'm sorry you're bored."

Ace drew a deep breath, inhaling her scent before

he relaxed against her.

"Tomorrow, we'll go on a good long ride." She tightened her hug for a minute, then gave him a pat and pulled back to look at his serious brown eyes. "Until then, you can watch me look for mice. How's that for excitement?"

Sam gave Ace's nose a kiss, then turned on the radio in the tack room and considered her job.

For as long as she could remember, Dad had talked about pouring a cement floor in the feed room. Until then, mice could burrow up from under the wooden floor in search of tasty grain.

Dad kept grain and corn in shiny aluminum garbage cans with tight-fitting tops. They should be mouseproof, but the mice remained hopeful some grain would be spilled or someone would be in a hurry and not wedge a lid on tightly.

While she worked, Sam's mind gnawed on her own problem.

Where was the Phantom? What would Slocum do if the stallion he'd always wanted was nearby? She'd looked away from him so Rachel wouldn't see him and tattle.

But looking away had worked too well. When she'd looked back, the Phantom had vanished. Was he still on the ridge trail above the Gold Dust? Would whatever lured Rachel up there in the first place make her return and notice him?

Sweating and troubled, Sam was trying to distract

herself by singing along with the radio when she heard footsteps.

Dallas stood in the doorway. Just behind him, stood Ace.

"Sam, you're going to have him right in here with you if you let him wander like this. It's a bad habit." Dallas shooed Ace with a brush of his hand, and the gelding drew back, insulted. "If a lid's ever left off one of these cans, he could get in here and eat himself to death."

Sam knew it was true. Horses were grazing animals. Most would eat as long as there was food.

"But I didn't let him out."

"The inside corral gate is open and unlatched. And here he is," Dallas said.

Sam approached Ace and touched his neck as if he had the answer. He probably did, but he just swished his tail and looked up at the rafters.

"I did hug him," Sam admitted. "But I didn't go inside the corral, so I couldn't have left the gate open, even accidentally."

Dallas gave her a frown full of disappointment.

"Well, who'm I supposed to believe, Samantha? You or my lyin' eyes?"

Even if Dallas's arthritis was making him cranky, he had a point.

"I'm sorry," she said, and hustled Ace back into his pen.

Sweetheart gave them both a scolding look.

"Yes, you stayed in like a good girl," Sam told Gram's pinto. "But how did this bad boy get loose?"

She considered the inside latch. It was open, all right. She supposed Ace might have rubbed against it, scratching an itch, until the latch opened. Or it was barely possible Gram had forgotten to lock the pen when she put Sweetheart inside.

With both latches in place, Sam tugged at the gate from outside. It held.

Ace nudged the finger she shook at him. He knew she was joking. "No kidding, Ace. Don't go getting us both in trouble."

Just after midnight, a horse woke Sam. She sat up in bed, fingers curled into her quilt, waiting for the sound to come again.

A joyous whinny drifted through the night. She knew it was Dark Sunshine because she'd heard that sound before. When the mare first came home from running with the mustangs, she'd used that same greeting to Popcorn.

But Popcorn and Dark Sunshine were both in the ten-acre pasture.

Sam's heart thudded. It was him.

Cautious not to make a sound, she slipped from bed and tiptoed downstairs. The stove clock and refrigerator hummed in the dark kitchen as Sam let herself out into the night.

Across the ranch yard, Blaze stood and shook.

Then he decided he was too sleepy to come along, and flopped back down.

Good. Sunny's racket was enough to wake Dad and Gram, but they might roll over and go back to sleep. If Blaze started barking when he saw the Phantom, they'd both be up and notice she wasn't in bed.

The moon was a smudged thumbprint, offering little light, but Sam had made this midnight expedition to the river often enough that she knew where to place her bare feet to avoid rocks. The dirt underfoot felt powdery and warm, and though it made for easy walking, it felt wrong.

Not wrong, she told herself, just bad weather for ranching.

Even though she couldn't see the Phantom, she knew he was there. When she reached the bank, Sam stopped and waited.

She could hear cattle lowing not too far away.

River Bend's white-faced Herefords had made their way out of the sage-covered foothills, closer to the main ranch and the river. Beyond the mooing cattle, Sam heard nothing. And there was no sign of the Phantom.

For a minute, she watched stars sparkle on the river's rills. Then she closed her eyes. If her sight adjusted to the darkness, she might see him.

When her eyes opened, Sam saw a flicker on the far riverbank. Like a pure, white wing, the Phantom's mane flared away from his neck.

Sam held her breath until it hurt. Tonight, he was magical. The moon emerged just for him, making the stallion's coat shimmer with silver light.

Gone was the mischievous horse who'd played hide-and-seek with her on the ridge trail that afternoon. Tonight the Phantom hadn't uttered a sound, yet he'd pulled her to the river.

Only one thing puzzled Sam. Why wasn't he wading toward her?

She grabbed a handful of nightgown in one hand, held it clear of the water, and started forward.

Usually, the stallion met her halfway. The first time she'd mounted him, as a colt, she'd done it in this river. She believed that memory made him return here. But tonight, he made her come to him.

Sam was shocked by the shallow water. Halfway across, it barely reached the middle of her shin, and it was tepid, warmed through by the day's sun.

That's when she knew she could wade all the way across. La Charla was only about a city block wide, and tonight the current was sluggish and slow.

Now she heard the thud of his hooves, trotting down the bank, wheeling, and trotting back.

Sam slogged closer. She should feel dumb, wandering so far from home in her white nightgown. What if she fell and broke her leg? But she didn't feel dumb, just entranced, like a sleepwalker called from bed to do something important.

Sam didn't look back. If the porch light was on

and Dad or Gram was watching, she was already sunk. Better to have time with her horse than get in trouble and not even get a chance to touch him.

She didn't slip on the rocks underfoot. When she reached the other shore, the Phantom stood off and watched her. Sam lowered her eyes, wringing out the hem of her nightgown, even though she'd have to wet it again going home. As she twisted the water out in a splatter on the parched ground, she heard the stallion come closer.

Warm breath sighed over the nape of her neck. Sam shivered as gooseflesh raced down her arms.

Veiled by a thick forelock that parted only over his eyes, the stallion settled back as Sam straightened.

"Hey, boy," she crooned to him. "C'mere boy."

The stallion blinked but didn't come within reach.

"Do you think I was ignoring you this afternoon, hmmm? Is that why I'm getting the cold shoulder?"

The stallion stretched out his nose, then jerked it back, shaking his head.

"I was trying to keep Rachel from seeing you, that's all. She's kind of a nutcase, boy, and if she knew you were right there on their ranch, who knows what would happen."

Sam remembered Linc Slocum's voice, bragging about his deal with a rodeo stock contractor. For one ugly instant, she imagined the Phantom exploding out of a bucking horse chute into an arena filled with cheers and music.

That would be illegal, of course. The Phantom was a free-roaming mustang, and it would be against the law for Slocum to capture, sell, or trade him to Karla Starr. But Slocum had proven before that he placed his own desires above the law.

As the image of a high-spurring cowboy faded from her imagination, Sam noticed that the Phantom stood beside a boulder just the perfect height for a mounting block.

The Phantom didn't belong to her, either. But once he had. And tonight he seemed lonely and almost tame. Temptation told her the stallion might let her ride him into the night.

"One day, a long time ago, you let me on your back, boy." Sam edged closer. "You know I wouldn't hurt you."

The stallion flicked his ears but trusted her to come closer.

As she put one foot on the rock, the Phantom turned to watch. When both feet were up, Sam bit her lip.

"Zanzibar . . ." She sighed his secret name and the stallion answered with a nicker.

A wild horse shouldn't be so trusting. She wouldn't try to climb on tonight.

But if she only did it once . . .

No night birds called. La Charla ran as quietly as unfurled satin. The entire world held its breath, waiting to see what she would do.

"Zanzibar, could I try? Please? You know I won't hurt you."

Sam leaned one palm on the stallion's back. It felt smooth and muscular. She placed her other hand there, too, then smoothed her hands together along his back.

The Phantom sidled just out of reach. Sam felt her chest deflate.

"Not tonight?"

As if he understood her disappointment, the stallion lowered his head. His lips whuffled along the ground as if he'd lost something, and Sam knew just what it was. For a minute, they'd both lost their good sense.

Then, just like the playful colt he'd once been, the Phantom surprised her. Head still lowered, he grabbed the ruffle at the hem of her nightgown and tugged until the ruffle ripped.

Then the stallion released the fabric and shook his head.

For the space of three heartbeats, he rubbed his velvet muzzle against her neck. He uttered a deep nicker that was so much like language, Sam tried to understand the words.

And then he trotted away. Light as a ghost horse, he drifted over a series of trails and shortcuts up the mountainside.

By road, the way to the Phantom's valley took close to four hours. Riding Ace and following the

Phantom's path, Sam had made it once in two.

She wanted to follow him. Instead, Sam watched the silver stallion until he was out of sight. She didn't cross back to River Bend until even the sound of his passage had died into silence.

Finally, she walked home. With each step away from him, Sam felt a tearing in her chest. Her head believed it was time to go back to bed, to pretend the night hadn't been interrupted by magic. But her heart knew better.

Together, she and the Phantom had woven a spell that let them read each other's minds. And tonight, Sam had the awful feeling that the stallion had been saying good-bye.

Chapter Four ❧

Ƨhe didn't get caught returning to her room on Saturday night, but Monday afternoon was a different story.

Journalism was Sam's last class of the day and her busiest. Mr. Blair expected the Darton High *Dialogue* to be a real newspaper, so he treated students like real reporters. If they didn't turn in daily homework, meet deadlines, and follow the direction of student editors, they didn't get "paid" with passing grades.

The classroom buzzed with the sound of tapping computer keys, rustling papers, and a ringing phone, but Sam often escaped to the photo lab.

Eerie red light that wouldn't damage exposed film glowed over the darkroom sinks where Sam developed the film she'd shot for a story about overcrowded classes. Little string "clotheslines" held wet prints of Friday night's football game.

In spite of the smelly chemicals used to develop the film, Sam smiled at her handiwork. Everything about photography was fun. She loved getting down on the football field, far closer than the fans and cheerleaders, and crouching to catch the action with her camera. When grunting players crashed into each other, the ground shook as it did when wild horses galloped.

Sam stared at the sink before her. There was a different sort of excitement to this moment. In an almost supernatural way, images turned from vague blotches into pictures.

It was quiet inside the darkroom. The revolving door, designed to keep light from invading, grated as it opened, acting as an alarm.

She was expecting the sports editor, who was itching to see if Sam had caught a particularly great run by a lumbering linebacker, so she didn't glance up from her work when she heard the door turn.

"This seems a place where we'll have a bit of privacy."

The British accent gave her away. It was Rachel. Why would the rich girl want to talk with her in private?

Unless, Sam speculated, Rachel planned to get rid of witnesses to the disgrace of ripping her designer jeans and skinning her knees.

"What's up?" Sam asked as she sneaked a glance at Rachel's knees. It was easy to do, since Rachel wore a plaid sundress that barely reached mid-thigh.

But the uncertain red glow in the darkroom showed no harm to Rachel's knees. Of course not.

"I want you to put some polish on my riding skills."

"What?"

"Yelping isn't necessary, Samantha, and there is some need for secrecy," Rachel scolded.

Sam's head was spinning. She would have been less surprised if Rachel had tried to drown her in the sink.

"You want me to teach you to ride?"

"I know the basics. What I need is practice under the eye of someone who can point out ways I can improve. This is important to me."

A little flattered, but still confused, Sam asked, "But why?"

"Did I not say this was important to me?"

"That's not really a reason."

"Let's say *that* information is available on a need-to-know basis." Rachel smirked. "And no one—certainly not you—needs to know."

"Then you don't need my help," Sam said. "Hire someone who does it for a living."

She turned back to her work. The print in the sink was almost ready when Sam realized temper had dictated her words.

What a mistake. Slocum would probably pay her big bucks to teach his princess to ride.

"But I want you to work with me," Rachel said.

That made Sam look up. The reddish light made Rachel's lower lip look even glossier as she pouted.

"You don't even like me." Sam noticed Rachel didn't rush to correct her. "And you don't like horses."

"I must find a way to make this work." Rachel mused to herself. She steepled her glittering bronze fingernails together and pointed to Sam. "You don't have to be very good, just inexpensive."

Sam laughed. "You don't have much experience at kissing up, do you?"

"You needn't act insulted. We both know I could have a superb horse master. Which you are not. However, I must clear purchases over a certain amount with my father."

"So, do it."

"I would." Rachel's face brightened. "Except this is a surprise."

It made sense, Sam supposed. Still, she didn't want to hang around with Rachel. Even in a corral.

Rachel was selfish, conceited, and rude. Sam admired nothing about her. Then she flipped her fingers through her own growing-out cap of hair and looked at the smooth sweep of Rachel's. Almost nothing.

"The only people who'd know about it wouldn't matter," Rachel said.

That meant Gram, Dad, Jake, and Jen. How

could Rachel believe they didn't matter? And even if she believed it, why would she say it?

"But Jake doesn't like me," Rachel went on sounding incredulous. "And if he should hear I made the tiniest mistake, it would be just like him to tell his gang of friends—not that I care what *they* think," Rachel hurried to correct any conclusion Sam might jump to. "But word spreads." Rachel's smile said she felt a little sorry for herself. "Some of us are always the focus of other people's attention."

Yeah, it's real tough being you, Sam thought. But she didn't say it. She was too busy trying to figure out what Rachel was up to.

The story didn't hang together. Sure, Linc Slocum would be happy if his daughter fit into his Western fantasy, but Sam couldn't believe Rachel cared about pleasing him.

"You know that becoming a good rider means work, and getting your hands dirty, maybe even sweating," Sam said.

Rachel didn't rise to the bait. Instead she put on an even more superior tone. "May I be blunt, Samantha?" She didn't wait for permission. "This drought has been tough on all the small ranchers and it's bound to get worse. Some will certainly lose their property. The pay I give you for this may not help a lot, but the good opinion of my father will."

Someone in the other room tapped on the revolving door and shouted, "Sam? Got those photos yet?"

"In a minute," Sam called, but she was thinking about what Rachel had just said.

This didn't fit with Rachel's personality, either. She cared about makeup and MTV, occasionally about winning a school election, but not about weather and agriculture.

"Why would you be paying attention to the drought?"

Rachel gave a half-smile as she walked her fingers along the edge of the developing sink. "Just how do you think my daddy got so rich? You don't know, do you?"

"No, I don't. How?" Sam asked.

"Keep wondering, little cowgirl." Rachel patted Sam's cheek and headed for the door. "But don't take too long. The title 'Best in the West' will be mine by June."

Even though she hated to do what Rachel told her, Sam kept wondering all afternoon. It probably slowed down her after-school chores, too, because by the time she had Ace saddled to go ride with Jen, Dad and the hands were riding in from the range and dusk was hovering over the hills.

All four men looked tired and unhappy.

Ace gave a little buck as Pepper and Ross turned their horses out into the big pasture. Usually, they'd tease her. Today, neither seemed to notice. Dallas rode by on Tank. Too weary for a greeting, he just raised a hand and smiled.

Dallas's smile wasn't really for her. It was for the horse he was leading, his old gelding, Amigo. The bay's muzzle was frosted with white and his eyes looked hazy, but he was the best horse Dallas had ever owned. The only horse he'd trust with his life, Dallas always said.

And that's why, on the gelding's twenty-fifth birthday, he'd been turned out to pasture. Only once in a while did bad range conditions force Dallas to bring him in.

Dad drew alongside Sam, on Banjo. His face was grimed with dust.

"Gettin' kind of a late start," he said.

"I know, but I'll be back in time for dinner. And my algebra homework." Sam made a face and Dad managed a smile. "I spent a lot of time with Sunny," she told him. "I don't know if she'll ever settle down."

They glanced toward Dark Sunshine. The mare seemed determined to make Sam wrong. She grazed with the saddle horses as if she'd been born among ropes and fences.

Across the yard, Blaze gave a sharp yap and ran circles around the cowboys as they stomped dirt from their boots outside the bunkhouse.

It was a sight Ace saw daily, but he shied as if Blaze were a werewolf. Sam slipped in the saddle. Embarrassed, she steadied herself.

"Quit that," she scolded Ace.

"It's a lot of work taming a mustang," Dad agreed. "They're always lookin' for trouble. And if it's not there, they'll imagine it."

Sam knew he was talking about Ace as well as Sunny. Dad might be right, but mustangs had to take care of themselves on the range. Of course they watched for danger.

"If you plan to keep that buckskin, gentle her. Otherwise, what's to keep her from passing her wildness on to her baby? Or coming at us hoof and teeth if she needs help foaling?" Dad shook his head. "You better plan on handling the young one all the time."

"You bet," Sam said.

Her heart went zinging skyward at the thought of a wobbly-legged foal with Sunny and the Phantom for parents.

"No daydreamin'," Dad said. "Go work the *loco* out of Ace and get back here in time for dinner. I smell fried chicken, and I'm hungry enough to eat it all, then lick the platter clean."

When she finally met up with Jen, Sam's mind was spinning.

She didn't like keeping secrets from Jen. They were best friends, and that meant sharing everything.

Well, almost everything. As Ace and Silly zigzagged around clumps of sagebrush, Sam decided she and Jen did the same. They detoured around a few private spots. Jen knew Sam had found the Phantom's hideout, but she didn't ask where it was. And though Sam knew Jen's parents fought too much, she didn't ask for details. Both girls considered those topics off-limits—unless there was an emergency.

In the darkroom, Rachel had said there was "some need for secrecy" about her riding lessons. She'd mentioned gossip, and that wasn't a problem with Jen. But what if Rachel was really worried about something else? Sam felt like growling. It wasn't that she felt loyal to Rachel, but this wasn't her secret to tell.

Sam abandoned her thoughts as a shadow suddenly crossed between her and Jen. Both girls looked up.

A red-tailed hawk soared overhead. The bird's rasping scream gave Sam chills. She'd never heard anything like it in the city. The sound was everything she'd missed about Nevada when she lived with Aunt Sue in San Francisco.

"Let's follow her," Jen said. Blond braids flapping and glasses slipping down her nose, Jen set Silly into a lope.

The girls rode together, keeping the bird in sight to see where she'd nested.

"If she drops a feather, I get it," Sam said.

"For a good luck charm or something?" Jen asked.

"It's almost Jake's birthday." Sam paused. Jen

was listening hard, frowning to hear over the clattering hooves.

"Jake wants a feather for his birthday?" Jen asked.

"No." Sam laughed. "But how cool would it look braided into Witch's mane with the new headstall I got him?"

"Wow," Jen agreed. Then she frowned. "She's getting away."

They galloped, rushing into a wind that tasted of sagebrush and rabbitbush and something tangy Sam couldn't name. The horses ran side by side, surging after the hawk.

If a russet feather fell, Sam knew she would give it to Jake, but she longed to keep it for just a while. Holding a little piece of wildness—not stolen from an animal, but freely given—always filled her with quiet wonder.

But the hawk didn't care what Sam wanted. After leading them on a swooping path toward War Drum Flats, the red-tail made a shrugging motion with her wings, banked upwind, and disappeared into the evening sky.

"We've lost her," Jen said.

"I know, and I've got to get home."

"Me, too. D'you want to let these two drink a minute before we go?"

"Sure."

The horses followed a well-worn path past a

tumble of boulders, toward a dirt road that paralleled the highway. Few vehicles used the road, since it dead-ended near the narrow mountain trail up to Lost Canyon.

The pond was in sight when Jen's palomino reared.

Chapter Five ∾

The palomino stood tall, white-stockinged front legs flailing in surprise.

"Silly!" Jen shouted. She slammed forward on the mare's neck, forcing her to touch down. "She smelled something, I think. Did you see how she was flaring her nostrils?"

Sam shook her head and stayed focused on Ace. The gelding danced with uneasiness as he watched Silly.

"It's okay, boy," she assured him, but as soon as she saw Jen regain control of Silly, Sam twisted in her saddle, searching for whatever had frightened the horses.

Could it be the Phantom? Sam's glance swept the area around the pond, the path to Lost Canyon, and the giant stair-step ridges and buttes that hid deer trails and passages to the stallion's hideaway.

The stallion and his herd weren't in sight. Neither

were antelope, coyotes, snakes, or even a sage hen that might have startled Silly. What else could the palomino have smelled?

Sam knew she and Jen paid attention. Even hurrying, they would have noticed signs of danger. Jen was probably right. It was a sound or scent beyond human senses.

Ace snorted, telling Sam he found her fidgets far from comforting. He shifted his weight to his hind legs before teeter-tottering away from the earth, threatening to rear.

One horse rearing was a mistake. Two horses rearing was an unplanned rodeo, and Sam wanted no part of it.

Using leg pressure and a kick, Sam forced Ace to walk, then trot. Awkwardly, he went.

"That's it, keep going." Sam kept after Ace with her voice and hands. As long as the gelding moved forward, he couldn't rear, so she rode him right into the water.

The pond was shallow and the footing gummy. Ace's hooves made sucking sounds until he stopped to drink. He'd be a muddy mess to clean up, but at least she was still in the saddle.

"What was that all about?" Jen had dismounted to let Silly drink. She stood beside the palomino, holding the reins in two places.

In seconds, both horses had drunk their fill of the cloudy water.

"You've got me." Sam rode Ace slogging out of the pond. His legs were coated with taupe-colored clay.

"These two are going to need a bath, not a brushing," Jen grumbled and remounted Silly.

All at once, Sam remembered Rachel's taunt about the drought. She hadn't been asked to keep that remark secret.

"Hey, Jen, how did Slocum make his money?"

The setting sun cast a gold glaze across the lenses of Jen's glasses as she tucked back hair which had escaped from a braid.

"Do you know?" Sam prodded.

"Of course. He gets it from people like my family."

"I don't understand," Sam said.

Jen took a deep breath and jiggled one foot in its stirrup. "My dad's been doing some research, and it seems like Slocum is buying up farms and ranches all over the West. He builds houses, malls, sometimes even factories."

Sam tried to unravel Rachel's threat. Of course she wouldn't want River Bend covered with acres of free parking, but Dad and Gram would never sell.

"Dad says Slocum is a genius at finding people in debt. A lot of times drought pushes them over the edge."

Sam felt chills at that suggestion.

"In Montana it was mad cow disease. It was just a

scare. The cattle turned out to have something like the sniffles, but the ranchers couldn't *give* that beef away."

It made sense, Sam thought. But Jen wasn't done talking.

"And you know how the ranchers all help each other out?"

"Sure," Sam said, "with roundups and haying and when we had the fire—"

"Well, if Rancher One sells out, he can't help Rancher Two with haying. Rancher Two hires a hay crew, goes broke paying them, and sells out. Then Rancher Three thinks, 'If I moved to the city, I could work nine-to-five in air-conditioned comfort and my kids could play soccer instead of watching barbed wire rust.'"

"Personally, I like watching barbed wire rust." Sam knew it was a weak joke, but she didn't have time to improve it. The horses had begun flicking their ears and acting restless again.

When Ace shied, Sam saw what he did.

She wheeled Ace, dismounted, and kicked at the dirt. Beneath a puff of dust, something glittered.

"What is it?" Jen asked.

Sam picked up the shimmering gold strand and examined it.

"Silky fringe," Sam said, "like you'd have on a fancy shirt or costume."

"*That* couldn't be what scared my big, strong palomino." Jen leaned forward and kissed Silly's neck.

"I don't think so either." Sam shoved it into a pocket as she remounted.

They rode in silence, squinting against waves of dust that came with each gust of wind, until they came to the spot where they usually parted to ride home.

Then, Jen cleared her throat.

"There's something I didn't tell you about Slocum," she said. "In one way it doesn't matter. In another way, it's really important."

"Okay." Sam found herself swallowing hard.

"The first ranch Slocum bought belonged to two families in Colorado who could trace their roots back to pioneers. They'd helped each other for over a hundred years. Some of their kids had even married, so after a while it was all one huge ranch. But they were in serious debt to the bank.

"Slocum made them an offer and they finally had to take it. And then Slocum sold the ranch to a beer-brewing company and made a ton of money." Jen gave a wry smile. "My dad says Linc has a nose for something dying, and he's no better than a land vulture. That's how he got our ranch."

Jen never cried, so Sam told herself it was probably just a reflection she saw on her friend's glasses. *Some small ranchers will certainly lose their property.* That's what Rachel had said.

Sam's heart hammered as she rode for home. She had to ask Dad if the River Bend Ranch was in danger.

＊ ＊ ＊

No one noticed she was late.

Showered and wearing satisfied grins, Dallas, Pepper, and Ross were just coming down the steps, leaving the house as Sam ran in from the barn.

That was weird. The cowboys took turns cooking in the bunkhouse kitchen, but they'd definitely looked well-fed.

When Sam eased into the house, the kitchen table was so laden with food, Gram and Dad were just looking at it.

Gram's usually tidy bun straggled down her back, but her hands perched on her hips and she looked proud.

"I'm trying out fried chicken recipes for the county fair cook-off," she told Sam. She gestured toward three plates that had probably been piled higher a few minutes before. "I've got their votes. Now, it's our turn."

Sam obeyed Gram's taste test rules, eating bites of mashed potatoes and green beans in between chicken sampling, but her full stomach couldn't chase away thoughts of Slocum.

"Time to vote," Gram said as Dad lay down his fork. "Which is best? The Buttermilk Crunch recipe . . ." Gram pointed to an empty pink plate. "Cha Cha Chicken." She indicated a dish holding a lonely red-flecked chicken wing. "Or Honey Fried?"

"Honey Fried." Dad placed his napkin on the

table as if offering surrender.

Gram turned to Sam.

"They were all really good," she said. "But if I have to pick just one, it's the Honey Fried for me, too."

Gram gave them a lopsided smile. "But that's my usual recipe. It's the one I always cook."

"Lucky us," Dad said. He leaned over and patted Gram's hand.

"How did Pepper, Dallas, and Ross vote?" Sam asked.

"Pepper gave half his vote to the Cha Cha Chicken, but otherwise, same as you," Gram said.

Before they left the table, Sam blurted her question. "How much trouble are we in from this drought?"

Dad's smile melted. "It hasn't helped, that's for sure."

"Really, Dad. Tell me how bad things are."

Dad glanced at Gram, then shrugged. "We've been this close to the edge many times. A lot depends on winter rainfall. We need it now, before all the topsoil blows away."

Sam thought of the curtains of dust she and Jen had ridden through today. "But we aren't farmers. Why is the soil important?"

"Graze for the cattle next spring, and then our hay crop to see us through next winter," Dad explained.

"Then, if rain comes all at once, like it does sometimes, even thirsty ground can't absorb it," Gram said. She looked toward the window. "We get flooding and it washes away what topsoil the wind left behind."

"It's kind of hard to know what to hope for," Sam said.

"Honey, you just leave the worrying to us," Dad said.

Gram nodded, but added, "I think it's a real sign of maturity that you're considering the future of your home, Samantha. It shows you're really growing up."

Gram placed a reddened and wrinkled hand on Dad's brown one. Together, those hands had done a hundred years of work. That struck Sam harder than Gram's compliment.

"What brought this on?" Dad asked.

Sam didn't rush to tell the truth. Once she did, she was committed to working for Rachel's money. And didn't *that* sound selfish?

"Rachel asked me to teach her to ride," she admitted.

"I thought she already knew how," Gram said.

Dad frowned, probably trying to see how this fit with Sam's worries.

"She said she'd pay me," Sam explained.

"That's fine, if you want to," Dad said.

"There'll be field trips coming up, and clothes you want to buy," Gram said. "If you earn money, it's yours."

Gram and Dad gave her smiles that said the small amount Sam earned wouldn't really help the ranch.

Still, she didn't know how to translate what Rachel had said about earning Linc Slocum's good opinion.

"Has Mr. Slocum ever tried to buy River Bend?" Sam asked.

Dad slid his chair back from the table with a screech. Even though Sam knew he wasn't mad at her, he looked scary.

"I'd carry this land bucket by bucket and dump it in the Pacific Ocean before I let him have it." Dad started from the kitchen, then turned back, voice even lower. "You can bet on that."

From the living room, Dad's chair creaked and the television came on louder than usual.

"We're good neighbors to the Slocums," Gram said, "because that's the way things should be. But when he came in here a couple of years ago, flashing his money around, some of us decided to stand firm.

"It was just after your accident, and Linc had the idea we'd want to sell and move out. Even made us feel ashamed for sending you off all alone to San Francisco." Gram looked up, her expression guilty.

"I had Aunt Sue," Sam protested.

"Of course you did," Gram said. "In any case, Linc went to the Potters, the Dennis family, the Greens, and the Kenworthys. Only the Potters and Kenworthys sold out, but—" Gram stood and picked up two platters. "This could be a hard year."

After the dinner dishes were washed and dried, Sam trudged upstairs to do homework.

Television didn't tempt her tonight. Not only did she have algebra homework, she was trying to figure out the history project Mrs. Ely had assigned.

But Sam's mind wandered. She placed the silky gold fringe on the desk beside her. Something more than this had frightened the horses. Glancing toward her bedroom door to make sure no one could see her, Sam raised the fringe to her nose and sniffed it herself. It might, very faintly, smell like incense.

She put it back down. Who had a shirt with gold fringe?

Slocum was the only neighbor who wore such showy gear for routine rides. Everyone else saved such finery for rodeo time.

The Darton rodeo had ended months ago, in June, but who knew how long the fringe had been out on War Drum Flats?

Sam forced herself to look at her algebra book. She positioned her paper beside it and copied a problem, neatly.

$3x + 11x =$

Sam looked away from the text and gave the fringe a poke with her pencil eraser.

This was so frustrating. She knew the fringe was a clue to something, but it remained a mysterious x to her.

Chapter Six ✎

The next morning, Sam was rubbing her hands together, wishing she'd worn her gloves to the bus stop, when Jen gave her a shove that spun her toward the mountains.

"Sam! Oh my gosh! Look!"

For an instant, all Sam saw was Jen's breath, hanging before her like smoke in the cold morning air. Then she saw what had startled her friend.

Hooves crunching dry earth, a band of mustangs swirled in an uneasy bunch. The lead mare nipped with flattened ears, keeping the horses on the wild side of the highway. Only the Phantom crossed.

The Phantom. What was he doing down here by the highway? Sam watched with amazement as he approached.

As if the asphalt might splinter beneath his hooves, the stallion took a step, stopped, and squared up. Faint tremors ran over him like water, but his ears pricked forward and his eyes were set on Sam.

She risked a quick glance away from the stallion, at Jen. Her friend watched her with awe and a little suspicion.

"He's coming to you," Jen said.

Sam opened her mouth, then closed it.

There was no use denying the statement. Jen knew horses. She knew the silver stallion wasn't wandering across the highway by chance.

Suddenly, the girls heard the labored downshifting of the school bus. It rumbled their way, with one more hill to crest, and then a dip. When it came up the other side, the bus would be just yards from their stop.

Fear lodged in Sam's throat. She couldn't speak and she struggled to take a breath.

The Phantom didn't notice. If he heard the diesel engine, he was too focused on Sam to pay attention.

A collision between tons of metal and delicate equine flesh flashed in Sam's imagination. She saw him rearing, falling . . . *She had to stop him.*

"Get back!" Sam shouted so loudly Jen flinched. "Hyah!" She waved her hands and bolted onto the pavement. "Get out of here!"

The stallion only cocked his head and considered her craziness. His white mane cascaded like a waterfall as he frolicked a step closer.

Jen joined her, yelling and jumping into the air.

They looked back and forth, searching for the

bus, staring at the confused horse.

The bus had dropped into the dip. Only an edge of yellow roof moved closer. In a minute, it would be upon them. Why hadn't the stallion spooked? What if the bus struck him?

Something like electricity rushed through Sam's bones and muscles. She shoved Jen back toward the bus stop and darted into the road. The engine's huff clogged her ears. As soon as the bus crested, the driver would see her standing in his path.

The horn blared, vibrating her insides, just as the stallion's hot shoulder brushed hers. Sam turned to see the Phantom's eyes edged with white, mouth agape.

Clumsy with fear, he almost fell as the bus braked. Scraping hooves and a grunt of effort proved the stallion was fighting to keep all four legs beneath him.

He spun, still skittering for balance, and ran for his herd.

Sam didn't watch the mustangs go. The bus driver stood in front of her, yelling.

"What were you thinking?" His hands flew skyward in frustration. "Of all the — It was a *horse*. Just a horse. I could have killed you."

For a second, the driver's hands covered his face. She'd really scared him, Sam thought, but when he looked up, his fear had been replaced by fury.

"I'm writing you up, Samantha. I'm giving you a citation that will have you in trouble so deep you won't be able to see out for months! Now, get on that bus!" He pointed as if sending her to her room.

Sam ran up the steps onto the bus. Jen clattered right behind her. From the corner of her eye, Sam noticed Jen had snagged both of their backpacks.

Jen was such a great friend—and Sam knew she was going to need one. Although the bus was filled with people she knew, their astonished faces didn't look sympathetic. Of the thirty kids on the bus, half were gawking, with their mouths wide open.

The driver slammed into his seat and pulled the doors closed. He glared into the mirror and addressed everyone sitting behind him.

"No more distractions," he commanded. "I want it quiet as a tomb. One peep out of anybody and there'll be a pack of you going to the principal's office. Got it?"

Though a resentful murmur rippled through the students, they knew better than to protest.

As the bus jerked back into motion, Sam's stomach rolled with nausea. She closed her eyes, but it didn't help. She made fists until her fingernails bit into her palms. Cold sweat gathered over her top lip, but wiping it away would only call attention to her distress.

She swallowed. Probably, she hadn't almost died. Probably, her mind had exaggerated the nearness of the silver grille on the front of the bus. Probably, Zanzibar would have run away in time.

When Jen's elbow hit her in the ribs, Sam felt as

if she'd been awakened. Sam blinked heavy eyelids and pushed her hair back from her eyes.

Jen had taken a lens-cleaning tissue from her backpack. Methodically, she polished her glasses, held them up for inspection, and let her eyes slide sideways to meet Sam's.

It's okay. Jen mouthed the words silently, then slipped her glasses back on.

Sam really hoped she was right.

By the time they reached school and got off the bus, Sam had to hurry to her locker. Her rush didn't keep her from noticing the eyes that followed her. Up and down the halls, kids from the bus were spreading gossip about the morning's excitement.

Later, when a student messenger interrupted Sam's history class to give Mrs. Ely a yellow office pass, everyone looked at Sam.

"Sam?" Mrs. Ely raised one eyebrow, and Sam guessed word of her misdeed hadn't had time to spread to the teachers' workroom this morning.

She almost enjoyed her walk to the office. Unlike her three-story San Francisco middle school, Darton High's single story framed a central courtyard. Sam crunched through yellow cottonwood leaves and looked up at the patches of blue sky showing between wind-torn white clouds.

Sam pulled her sleeves down. The breeze cut right through her cotton shirt, feeling like winter, but that was the least of her worries. If she'd known when she got dressed this morning that she'd be talking with the principal, she would've worn her newest jeans. Or maybe even a skirt.

It probably wouldn't have made any difference.

Mrs. Santos wore a businesslike beige suit and fooled with a clip-on earring as Sam entered the principal's office. Not until Mrs. Santos pointed her toward a chair did Sam notice the principal was on the telephone.

During her first week at Darton High, Sam had interviewed Mrs. Santos for the school newspaper. She'd found the principal to be a no-nonsense woman with a great sense of humor. Would she feel that way when she left Mrs. Santos's office this time?

Sam waited. With luck, Mrs. Santos would just lecture her. There was no reason, really, for Gram and Dad to find out about her reckless behavior.

They worried, and they blamed the Phantom for Sam's riding accident. Even though the stallion had been young, and had carried her weight for less than an hour, they blamed him for Sam's fall, for the kick that knocked her unconscious and kept her in the hospital for several weeks.

After that, Sam had been forced to live in San Francisco for two years, just to be near a hospital.

Since the day Sam had returned from San Francisco, Gram had been afraid the stallion would hurt her again. And if Dad thought Rachel's riding off into the mountains was a "stunt," what would he say about this?

Mrs. Santos hung up the receiver.

"Sorry," she said. Immediately, her eyes skimmed a form Sam knew was the citation. Mrs. Santos frowned, then pushed the form toward Sam. "Look at this."

Sam studied the undecipherable handwriting. She recognized her name and the word *horse*, but that was all.

"I can't read it," Sam said.

"Neither can I, and I've never had trouble reading one of Mr. Pinkerton's citations before." Mrs. Santos shook her head. "The man's driven a school bus for fifteen years. He doesn't get rattled easily. Tell me what happened."

Sam did. She left out the fact that she knew the wild horse she'd rescued.

"It's not like I'm ever going to do this again," Sam ended her explanation.

"No," Mrs. Santos agreed. "Not *this*."

Sam wasn't sure what the principal's emphasis meant. While Mrs. Santos wrote on the form, Sam checked the wall clock. She'd missed half of P.E. The bad thing was, it was one of only two classes she had with Jen. On the other hand, it was one of two classes she had with Rachel.

When Mrs. Santos finally put down her pen, Sam realized she'd been sitting with fingers crossed on both hands while she awaited the principal's decision.

"You'll need to apologize to Mr. Pinkerton—"

Sam found herself smiling and nodding before Mrs. Santos finished her sentence.

"—and find other transportation to school for two weeks."

"You mean, I can't ride the bus?"

"That's what I mean." Mrs. Santos glanced at the phone that had begun ringing behind her.

"But then my dad has to know," Sam said.

"That's right," the principal said.

Sam shook her head. "I'm going to be mucking out the barn until I'm twenty-one," she moaned.

Mrs. Santos laughed, picked up the telephone receiver, and waved Sam on her way.

The other girls were already jogging toward the locker room when Sam reached her P.E. class and fell into step with Jen.

"I'm not suspended," Sam said. "Except from the bus."

"Could be worse, but what are you going to do?" Jen used the hem of her gold tee-shirt to blot her face.

"You'll be the first to know. Hey, I've got to ask you something."

"Math or vet stuff?"

"What?"

"You must realize that you don't ask my opinion

about much of anything except your algebra class and horse medicine," Jen said over the slamming of gym lockers. "On everything else, you just rush blindly ahead."

"Wrong." Sam shook her head and lowered her voice. "Here's the thing: in the past few days, the Phantom has shown up where he shouldn't have. Before this he's never come near me when other people were around. Now, he's done it twice."

Jen nodded, encouraging Sam to keep talking.

"So," Sam whispered, "do you think he could be asking for my help?"

Jen finished dressing, then faced Sam. Jen's expression was owlish. "Would this be a bad time for me to suggest your attitude toward the Phantom is anthropomorphic?"

Sam crossed her arms. "No worse than any other time—if your plan is to make me feel dumb."

They left the gym and walked toward their next classes. Jen was taking so long answering, Sam wondered if she'd used the word on purpose and hoped Sam wouldn't ask what it meant.

"Well?" Sam said.

"It means you're crediting an animal with human feelings," Jen said gently.

"But he does love me, like Silly loves you. And he actually leaves his herd to come see me. And I've helped him before . . ."

"But does he know that?" Jen asked.

Exasperation made Sam's voice loud. "Of course—"

"Hullo, ladies," Rachel said, suddenly appearing beside Sam. "Am I intruding?"

"Later," Jen said, splitting off toward her class.

"Yeah," Sam said. She quickened her pace, but Rachel kept up. Finally, Sam glanced over at her.

Olive silk pants billowed around Rachel's legs. The matching pullover should have appeared rumpled. Instead, Rachel looked incredible. It just wasn't fair.

"About our business arrangement," Rachel began. "And please don't give my reputation a thought. Since we're keeping this quiet, it won't matter that some might think you're a bad influence." Rachel gestured toward the principal's office.

"You know what, Rachel?" Sam felt her anger building again.

"If this is a bad time, we can talk later," Rachel said.

"No, it's a fine time." Sam paused outside her classroom door. "But you see, I've been suspended from riding the bus. And that means I have to wait for someone to pick me up from school. There's no telling when Dad gets in from the range, and Gram can't always get away, either."

"Yes, yes, they work so hard." Rachel rolled her eyes. "But they won't leave you here. You're just saying that to be annoying."

"No, I'm not," Sam insisted. "Some days they can't drive all the way into town until after dark. It's that whole *work* thing, you know? Like Jake was talking about?"

"Ride home with him, why don't you?" Rachel suggested.

"He rides with his brothers, and the Blazer's already too full," Sam said.

Besides, even if they could squeeze her into the Blazer, there wouldn't be room for Jen. Though she was a little ticked at Jen right now for that anthropo— *whatever* remark, they were best friends. They did some of their best talking at the end of the school day, riding home. She didn't want to give that up.

"There's always Mrs. Ely," Rachel suggested. "She seems to like you."

"No." Sam knew Jake's mom would give her rides, but wouldn't she have to stay for meetings and stuff?

Sam ducked inside her class and left Rachel musing over some great idea Sam knew she'd hate.

Rachel ambushed Sam in the hallway just outside journalism.

"It's all settled," Rachel muttered as if she'd planned something shifty. After all, her cheerleader friend Daisy was in journalism, too. "You can ride in my car. Our housekeeper doesn't mind."

Once Sam had cooled off, she'd realized that all of

her mental vows to save the ranch were worth nothing if she didn't teach Rachel, take her money, and get
in good with Linc Slocum.

Next, it occurred to Sam that this wasn't an idle
wish for Rachel. She wanted this a lot, so Sam could
hold out for what she wanted, too. And what she
wanted most didn't have a single dollar sign attached.

"That'll be fine." Sam gave Rachel a minute of
relief before adding, "And since you drive right by
her house, you can give Jen a ride, too."

"Jennifer Kenworthy?"

Sam kept her sarcasm trapped behind closed lips.

"She hasn't been barred from the bus, surely?"
Rachel scanned the crowded hall. "Jennifer likes
riding the bus."

"Rachel, you've never been on a bus or you
wouldn't say that. No one likes the smell of old bana-
nas and sweaty socks, and even on a good day . . ."
The horror on Rachel's face stopped Sam. "You
haven't, have you? You've never been on a school bus
in your life!"

"The first few days you were in this class, you
were so nice and quiet," Rachel snapped. "Why don't
you—" Rachel's eyes closed and stayed that way, as if
she were counting to a hundred.

Eventually, she opened her eyes.

"I suppose it doesn't matter." Rachel smiled and
smoothed the wing of dark hair as if it had been dis-
placed by her temper, but Sam was pretty sure

Rachel hadn't noticed Daisy in the doorway dead ahead.

The cheerleader stared at her friend as if she couldn't be certain Rachel was actually conversing with Sam.

Sam made sure to raise her voice as they approached.

"Thanks, Rachel," Sam said, nudging her. "You're a pal."

Chapter Seven ❧

Sam and Jen embarrassed Rachel the minute they slid into the baby blue Mercedes after school.

"Hi, Mrs. Coley," Jen said as she fastened her seat belt in the backseat.

"Jennifer, it's good to see you."

The woman who turned away from the steering wheel had boyish short gray hair and a welcoming smile.

"Hi," Sam said, leaning forward with her hand extended. "I'm Samantha Forster. I've seen you drive by, but I don't think we've met." Sam often felt a moment of uncertainty about people she'd known before the accident. This time, Rachel's huffing didn't help, but Mrs. Coley's handshake couldn't have been friendlier.

"Nice to meet you, Samantha. I'm Helen Coley. I know your grandmother, Grace, from church."

Sam squirmed a little. Although both Dad and

Gram were devout people, they had an ongoing battle about church. Gram believed folks liked to join together with the minister to pray for rain. Dad thought it gave them false hope, no different from teasing winds, which blew through carrying the smell of wet grass and rain-slick rocks from some luckier place.

"Yes, ma'am," said Sam, but Mrs. Coley had already turned her attention to the parking lot crowded with teenage drivers.

Sam didn't feel smug about riding in Rachel's Mercedes. She felt misplaced and uneasy. Telling Dad and Gram she'd been kicked off the bus would be ugly. They'd blame the Phantom, of course. Just when they seemed reasonable about mustangs, their old-fashioned ranchers' stereotypes cropped up.

As they edged through the parking lot, Sam saw RJay, editor of the Darton *Dialogue*, strolling to his car. When he did a double take at the sight of Sam and Rachel riding together, Sam waved. Rachel might have wanted to fling herself to the car floor, but she only flattened her spine against the seat back as they left Darton High traffic behind.

Sam was just thinking how cool it would be to have a saddle made with the supple leather used for the Mercedes' seat covers, when the car phone rang.

Sam and Jen looked at each other. Since they couldn't cover their ears, they shifted away and pretended not to listen.

"Ryan!" Rachel's voice brimmed with happiness, and though Sam knew she'd heard the name before, she couldn't place it until Rachel said, "What's up in Nottingham?"

Her brother, Jen mouthed, and Sam gave a tiny nod.

"Of course, Ry." Rachel's voice returned to its usual mocking tone. "My equitation instructor is in the Mercedes with me now."

Rachel's fingers flipped through her silky hair as she shifted with discomfort. "Anyone can improve. My skills will be top-notch for summer competition—Oh, it is not. It's no more a beauty contest than your steeplechasing."

She laughed at her twin's answer, then turned farther away from Sam and Jen and lowered her voice.

"Just the recognition. I'll donate the scholarship to the needy or something. That's what I was about to say. You always—" She paused, listening. "The advantage of being twelve minutes older, yes?"

Rachel's chat turned brittle again. "My horse? I'll let that be your summer surprise."

During the silence that followed, Sam decided Rachel didn't have a mount of her own. Of course, Linc wouldn't allow that to be a problem for long.

"Not really!" Rachel's gasp was so sudden, even Jen, who'd been politely pretending to study, glanced up at Rachel's suddenly red face.

"Christmas?" Rachel pronounced the word as if she'd just learned it. "She is?" Rachel sighed, and though her coloring faded toward normal, her expression was sad. "Switzerland. How nice. Well, then, of course you—and I guess you'll get to see my horse a little sooner than expected. Still, I want to surprise you, Ry. Okay, yes. Ta to you, too. I miss you."

Face to the window, Rachel curled against her side of the car, looking small.

No. Sam would *not* let herself feel sorry for Rachel. She couldn't forget the girl had dropped one of Mr. Blair's cameras and let Sam take the blame. And what about Rachel's mocking laugh as she said Sam looked like a boy? As if that weren't enough, Rachel had also been rude to Jake and Jen, Sam's two best friends in the world.

"Well, cowgirl," Rachel said suddenly. "My schedule's changed and so has yours. You'll give me the intensive course. Starting tomorrow, I'd say, since I must be riding well by Christmas. And you'll need to help me find an appropriate horse."

Rachel's lips formed a witchy smile, as if Sam had no choice.

As she replaced the car phone, Sam considered Rachel's unprotected back. Sam didn't think of herself as a violent person, but if Jen's knee hadn't nudged hers meaningfully, she might have explored her desire to give Rachel a punch.

The car's rolling tires were the only sound for a minute.

"Mother calls Ryan the conscience of the family," Rachel said.

Sam imagined Rachel with a cartoon devil perched on one shoulder, an angel on the other. If that was Ryan's duty, he was slacking. Linc and Rachel needed him, big time.

"I want your assistance, too," Rachel said to Jen.

Jen closed her book. "I'm fascinated," she said. "But it depends on what you need."

Rachel wrestled with whether she could admit she *needed* anything from them, then decided to let it go.

"Samantha knows," Rachel said.

"Sort of. You want to improve your riding skills."

Jen's hand couldn't cover her mouth before a laugh escaped.

"I have some skills," Rachel protested.

"What's the competition you want to enter?" Sam asked. "Is it the 'Best in the West' you mentioned the other day?"

"You want to be a rodeo queen?" Jen blurted.

The Mercedes slowed as if Mrs. Coley's foot had faltered on the gas pedal.

Rachel considered her green-gold-tinted fingernails.

"Karla Starr encouraged me to enter." Rachel's chin lifted as if the rodeo contractor's opinion was all that mattered. "Once I told Ryan, it became a fact. But I want to keep it a secret from Dad."

"My mom was first runner-up for Best in the

West, like, twenty years ago," Jen said, shaking her head. "I don't know, Rachel. You'd have to compete in horsemanship, modeling, and there's a personal interview."

"Riding is only a third of it." Rachel shrugged. "Plus, it would stop Ry from bragging about his silly water jumps, and I *have* been told—by an expert, mind you—that winning would be a piece of cake for me."

The day he'd come to River Bend for help, Slocum had mentioned Rachel had been perturbed ever since Karla Starr's visit. Rachel must have seen Champ, saddled and tied, and decided to prove to herself that she could still ride.

Had she made it as far along the ridge trail because she remembered how to ride, or because Champ was a patient, well-schooled horse?

"It would have worked out nicely," Rachel said, "if I'd had the whole school year to train. But Ryan's coming home at Christmas."

Sam felt a pulse of excitement. If Rachel's sense of urgency made her buckle down and work, they might finish sooner.

But was that a good thing? River Bend needed the money.

What would Rachel pay for lessons? Twenty dollars per hour? Thirty? Fifty? Sam knew she could earn enough money to help. She was adding up dollars and basking in possibilities, when Rachel sighed.

"I could pretend I was sick or tell him I'd changed

my mind," Rachel suggested.

"Come on, Rachel," Sam said. "You're not a quitter."

"Certainly not," Rachel said, but she looked surprised.

"If we got together three times a week after school, you'd make progress fast." Sam couldn't believe she'd volunteered to spend so much time with Rachel.

"That's a splendid idea, Samantha, perhaps the best you've ever had."

The shocked expression on Jen's face would have made Sam stop, but River Bend Ranch was at stake.

As they approached War Drum Flats, Sam saw a bachelor band of mustangs.

"Mrs. Coley," she blurted, "if it's not too much trouble—"

Everyone in the car followed Sam's pointing finger.

"Samantha, really," Rachel moaned, but Mrs. Coley was already pulling over.

"I'm another of those ranch women who actually likes mustangs," Mrs. Coley said. "I've been watching this bunch for a week or two."

"Are we in a time warp?" Rachel said. "It's taking forever to reach home."

In spite of Rachel's complaint, the Mercedes stopped at the roadside.

Shoulders touching, manes blowing, three young

stallions clung together so closely, Sam thought she could measure across all three chests with her out-flung arms.

Little bachelor bands like this one were common. When a lead stallion saw them as potential rivals for his mares, he used hooves and teeth to drive young males from the herd. Wandering the range, lonely and yearning for the safety they'd always known in a band, the young stallions formed small herds of their own.

"I call them New Moon, Yellow Tail, and Spike," Mrs. Coley confided.

The first name gave Sam chills. During the new moon, the sky was black. This colt had no white markings. Neither had the Phantom as a colt. In fact, as a two-year-old, he'd looked much like this leggy horse.

Distracted by memories, Sam took a minute to see how well the other young outcasts matched Mrs. Coley's names for them.

Spike had to be the bay whose mane stuck up almost as if it had been roached, then moussed into place. The sorrel, standing in the middle, had a long flaxen tail that really did look almost yellow. In spite of the warm fall temperatures, both were getting fuzzy winter coats. Only the black, who led the others by a half stride, still shone like glass.

As Sam watched, the black broke away from the others. He arched his neck and executed a sort of bow, inviting his pals into a mock battle.

Like guys sparring because they had nothing better to do, the three pulled each others' manes and tails. They reared and fenced with their front legs, clearly playing.

Sam had seen the Phantom fight a blue roan stallion she'd called Hammer, and this was different. The bachelors were practicing. One day they'd challenge another stallion for his harem. This was a study session for that day.

"If you could have your pick—" Jen began.

"The black," Sam answered without hesitation. "There's something about him . . ."

Sam's voice trailed off as her mind recognized what her eyes had already noticed.

The black was from the Phantom's herd, perhaps even his son.

Weeks ago, he and several other horses had been trapped by rustlers using Dark Sunshine for bait. The captive mustangs had very nearly been sold for pet food. Detective work and luck had rescued the horses, and they'd been released in the Phantom's territory.

But maybe his absence made the black seem an intruder and the Phantom had driven him away.

Done with their skirmish, the three horses rolled in the mud until they were caked with it.

"How gross," Rachel said. "That black one was kind of pretty, before."

"It keeps off bugs," Jen explained.

"I'd think that was the least of their worries," Rachel said, yawning.

"What do you mean?" Sam tried to keep her voice light, but Rachel had hinted at something secret before. If it had anything to do with wild horses, Sam needed to know.

"With BLM and other people trying to catch them, I just think they'd better watch out," Rachel said.

The mustangs did seem more intent on playing than watching for danger, but Sam knew they could vanish in a heartbeat.

"If they're caught by anyone except BLM, that would be illegal." Jen studied Rachel. "You know that, right?"

Rachel sat back in her seat and gave a superior laugh.

"Of course, and I'll thank you not to lecture me, Jennifer, for the remainder of our little car pool."

When Jen's index finger stabbed her glasses back up her nose, Sam knew Jen was about to declare she didn't want to be part of this arrangement.

With the excuse of showing good manners, Sam tried to make Jen feel too guilty to desert her.

"Rachel, Mrs. Coley, thanks so much for giving me a ride," Sam said. "I'm going to be in trouble, but at least I won't have to ask Dad and Gram to drive me back and forth."

Sam winced as the River Bend bridge came into view. The last time she'd been in big trouble, Dad and

Gram had turned her into a virtual slave.

"You have no idea how hard it's going to be to tell them what I did. All day long, I've been thinking about the right way to put it."

"Oh, I think you'll be spared that, dear." Mrs. Coley looked up in her rearview mirror. Sam could only see her eyes, but they were sympathetic. "Mr. Pinkerton, the bus driver, has a little romance going with Junie. You know, the waitress at Clara's diner."

"Yes," Sam said, and even she could tell her voice was faint with fear.

"Well, when Jed came back from buying some fuses for me at the Alkali store this morning, he told me all about your wild horse escapade."

"Don't worry, Sam," Jen said. "My dad wouldn't pick up the telephone unless he had to report a fire. A big one. He sure wouldn't call and tattle on you."

"No, you're right, Jennifer, but he did have a cup of coffee with Dallas while he was there." Mrs. Coley sighed. "He told me how that Junie sure is a chatter-box. Fact is, Samantha, if I know, I expect your folks do, too."

Chapter Eight ∽

The minute Mrs. Coley let her out in the ranch yard, Sam crossed her fingers. It was just possible Dallas had decided to keep her secret.

She didn't worry too much about Jake. Although he'd probably heard gossip at school, he wouldn't pass it on to Dad. There was no sign of his brother's truck or Witch, so maybe she'd beat him to River Bend.

The entire ranch simmered silently in the afternoon heat. Even Blaze didn't come running to meet her.

When Sam opened the door, she saw Gram and Dad sitting together at the kitchen table. That meant a lecture was brewing, but Sam was more worried over the missing snack.

Every day, since the first day of school, Gram had put a plate of cookies on the kitchen table. Today there were none.

And Dad was home in the middle of the day.

Though this was a slow time of year for cattlemen, Dad rarely came home before dusk.

Sam shrugged out of her backpack and let it fall to the floor. If she could tell them about the money she'd be making for Rachel's lessons, and about arranging her own rides to school, it would show she wasn't irresponsible.

They didn't seem in a rush to start, so Sam did.

"I guess you heard," she said.

"About the stunt you pulled," Dad said. "Not about your penalty."

"I can't ride the bus for two weeks," Sam answered, "but I—"

"Mrs. Santos is too soft," Dad said.

"Or," Gram suggested, "she's left the punishment up to us."

"That *is* punishment," Sam insisted. She drew a breath to steady herself, but it came in all quavery. "Just so you know, I've arranged to ride with Rachel Slocum for those two weeks. Mrs. Coley will pick me up at the bus stop. Uh, Mrs. Coley says she knows you from church."

Gram nodded, but her eyes looked sad. "Seems you have no sense at all when it comes to that horse. Sakes, Samantha, how long has it been since you've known not to run into the middle of a street? That's something a child would do."

"Shamin' her's not going to help," Dad said. "The only thing that will is BLM taking that stallion off the range and shipping him somewhere for adoption."

Sam didn't realize her hands had flown up to cover her heart until Dad looked at them.

"You think that's harsh, but it's the truth. I never thought I'd say it, but I'm embarrassed by you, Samantha."

Sam closed her eyes.

"And I'm scared for you, too."

"Dad, you wouldn't have let him get hit by the bus, I know you wouldn't."

"No. I woulda tossed a rock to spook him off the road, not run into the path of a bus."

It seemed so simple when Dad said it.

"I didn't think—"

"That's just what I mean," Gram said. "You're a smart girl, but that horse does something to you."

"You're not doing him any favors," Dad said. "You know how to think like a horse, so ask yourself what he's thinking. Is he a pet or a wild animal? Does he trust you or his own instincts? Being confused in his thinking is gonna get him killed. Or captured."

Still standing, Sam swayed a little at the truth of Dad's words. The Phantom had had two close calls. Though BLM tried to protect all mustangs, they had only a handful of rangers to patrol the whole state.

Plenty of people had dreamed of catching the ghostly white stallion rumored to roam this range. But now they knew he really existed and Sam blamed herself for proving he was no myth.

"That stallion is depending on you for his safety," Dad said. "If you love him, let him go back to being wild."

"Okay," Sam said.

"To help you keep that promise," Dad said, "you're confined to this ranch. You go to school and home, and that's it."

Sam didn't ask for how long, but she thought of the Phantom coming to the river, waiting for her.

"No slipping out at night, either," Gram said. "Don't make me keep watch, Samantha. It's beneath you."

Sam felt as if all her energy had drained out of her fingertips, but she had one more thing to say.

"If it's okay, Rachel's going to come over and start taking lessons tomorrow. The money's for the ranch."

Gram started to protest, but Dad cut her off.

"Thanks," he said, and the simple word sounded almost like forgiveness.

Thunder rolled and Ace neighed for attention as Sam shooed the hens into their pen. All day they wandered, picking bugs and worms from their hiding places. Gram said happy hens laid more and better eggs, and they rarely had trouble with hawks.

Still, they didn't seem to mind returning to their coop, which was shaded by an old cottonwood tree.

The ranch yard was quiet once they'd fluttered back inside. Teddy was tied back by the barn, but

Jake was nowhere in sight and Dad had ridden out on Banjo. Right after their talk, he'd mentioned a couple of steers with runny noses. He wanted to check them before nightfall.

Another rumble sounded. At first, Sam thought it was more thunder. Or Dad herding steers across the bridge to be doctored. Instead, a white pickup truck was crossing the bridge. It looked like Brynna's.

Brynna Olson would be a welcome visitor today. Not only had the BLM manager been the first to suggest keeping the Phantom on the range to improve free-roaming herds, lately she could almost always make Dad smile.

But as the truck drew nearer, Sam saw it wasn't Brynna's. This vehicle was newer, and its doors were decorated with gold stars trailing copper streamers and the words "Starr Rodeo Productions."

It must be Karla Starr, the rodeo contractor, but what could she want? They didn't have Brahma bulls or unmanageable horses. By Dad's decree, every animal on this place worked. Even Dark Sunshine and Popcorn were part of the HARP program, working to teach at-risk teenagers the patience needed to work with wild horses. So what would bring Karla Starr to River Bend?

Along with curiosity, Sam felt a rush of excitement. For a long time, rodeo stock contracting had been a man's world, but Karla Starr was breaking in.

When Dallas walked out of the bunkhouse, Sam

wished he hadn't. Not only had the foreman told on her, she could tell by the way he fixed her with a grim look that he thought he'd done it for her own good.

And now, he was horning his way in on Karla Starr, when Sam knew she could have handled the meeting just fine.

The way Dallas moved was a reprimand for Sam's irritation. He was in pain, and Gram had explained that his arthritis was aggravated by pinched nerves, a crushed disk, and vertebrae rearranged by a life he shrugged off as "rugged."

Now he stood near the truck door, and Sam thought he was trying to get rid of Karla Starr.

"As Wyatt told you on the phone, ma'am, we just can't help you."

The woman climbed out of her truck anyway. She bowed a little to Dallas as if he'd welcomed her.

"Well, I heard through the grapevine that you've got title to a few mustangs, and sometimes they can make pretty good bucking horses." Karla Starr flashed a smile toward Sam.

"That's true," Dallas said, "but these horses are workin' a special sort of job."

As Dallas described the HARP program, Sam studied Karla Starr.

She was probably younger than she looked. About thirty, Sam guessed, but her body looked hard as a stick and her skin was leathery. Her eyes were a lively hazel, though, and they bounced from Dallas to

Sam to the ten-acre pasture, taking everything in.

And then there was her hair. Sam decided it was show business hair. It flipped away from her face in a sort of ruffle, and it looked as if Karla Starr had gone into a hairdresser's salon with a shiny new penny, pointed to its pinky-bronze glitter, and said, "That's it; I want my hair that color, exactly." And it was.

But it wasn't her hair that fascinated Sam. The thin woman wore a black shirt with curlicues of fancy stitching across the yoke. Below that, slanting down from her collarbone, were twin rows of gold fringe that shimmered and swayed with her every movement.

Sam knew that if she could run into the house and grab the glittering strand from her dresser, upstairs, she could prove the fringe on Karla Starr's shirt matched the one she'd found at War Drum Flats.

Karla Starr had been there, where the three bachelor stallions rolled in the mud, where Ace and Silly had shied with fear, but why?

The address on her truck door said Mesa Verde, California, but Karla Starr had been spending a lot of time in this part of Nevada.

"I see," the woman said, then glanced at her watch. "But don't rule me out. Even if you don't have any now, I want to get dibs on any broomtails too ornery to use with children."

"Someone's led you astray, Ms. Starr," Dallas said. "We only have two horses for that program."

"Which would those be?" Karla Starr turned to

Sam as if she'd just recalled she was there. "And you're the young woman who can talk to wild horses."

Karla's smile was warm and friendly, as if she wanted to give Sam a girlfriends-only hug.

"That's an exaggeration," Sam said, wondering where she'd heard it. She pointed to distract the woman. "The albino," Sam said, "and the buckskin are mustangs."

"She's a beauty." Karla Starr's eyes flicked over the horse. "Tiny for a bucking horse, though, and a little soft in the belly."

"She's in foal," Sam said.

"Too bad." Her expression faded. She glanced at her watch again, then lifted one shoulder in a shrug. "In my business, there's no such thing as a long-term investment."

"Aw now, do you mean to say you don't breed bucking mares to bucking stallions?" Dallas asked.

"Never. I buy rough stock, buck 'em out, and resell when they lose their edge. A mare might go through her entire rodeo career before that one's ready for the arena."

Sam met Dallas's eyes. Neither of them knew what to say.

"And the albino?" Karla Starr raised one brow. "He's tall enough, but he doesn't have the look. Still, there's no telling what he'd do in the arena, properly prepared."

"Properly prepared with drugs, shocks, burns—"

Dallas used a casual tone for such horrors, but Karla Starr stopped him.

"Of course not. Those are tricks from the old days."

"Not so old," Dallas said. "When I worked for Slim Perkins, he was the only man raising stock instead of buying outlaws and terrifyin' them into bucking."

"I thought Slim Perkins was dead." Karla Starr laughed.

"He is, ma'am." Dallas looked hurt.

Why didn't Karla Starr go keep whatever appointment had her checking her watch every couple of minutes? There was nothing for her here.

"I can guarantee you my animals love to buck," the woman said, as if realizing she'd alienated them both. "It's play for them. Who wouldn't like a job where he only worked a couple of weekend afternoons a month?" She winked at Dallas. "Wouldn't take too long to get the cricks out of your back that way, would it?"

Dallas wasn't taken in. "These are lifelong cricks, ma'am, and I love my life the way it is. Just like these ponies do."

Karla Starr smiled as if she were indulging Dallas, then she looked past Sam and raised her auburn penciled eyebrows in surprise. "Well, now, who's this?"

Sam heard hooves right behind her. They were

determined, but not collected like a horse under saddle. Even before she saw him, she knew it was Ace.

"Hey, runt," Karla Starr said, pretending to joke with the gelding. "What're you up to? Is he just an old pet?" She reached to touch Ace's nose and he swung his head away.

"He's one of the best usin' horses on the spread," Dallas said. "He's a little spoiled, but—"

"Babying animals ruins them," Karla interrupted, grabbing on to something she and Dallas had in common.

How had Ace escaped his corral again? Sam couldn't figure it out, but when he nuzzled her palm, she let him.

"You spoil him with sugar cubes," Karla said.

"Almost never," Sam said.

"He's sayin' otherwise." Karla laughed, then sneaked another glance at her watch before looking toward the range.

"He's not supposed to wander," Sam agreed. "But since school started, he hasn't been getting as much work as he needs and he's been getting out of his corral."

"An escape artist." Karla looked at Ace with new eyes. "Usually means they're pretty smart."

A torrent of wind slashed through the ranch yard and Karla's copper curls blew in her eyes. She looked ready to go, and then Dad came loping across the bridge into the yard.

"Now, there's a horse," Karla said.

Dad rode Banjo, and the Quarter horse looked great. Collected and gleaming on his neck and shoulders, the gelding was all a working horse should be.

Karla Starr could just eat her heart out, Sam thought, because Dad would never sell Banjo.

"I should probably go, but I'd really like it if you could introduce me to your dad first."

Karla caught Sam's questioning look and laughed.

"I knew because you two look just alike," she said.

Sam motioned for Dad as he brought Banjo down to a trot. Dad looked impatient, displeased to have company, and downright peeved over Ace.

"Mr. Forster, I'm Karla Starr," she said before Sam could perform an introduction. "I love that gelding you're riding. He'd make a great pickup horse—"

"Excuse me." Dad made an apologetic gesture. "Samantha, what is Ace doing loose?"

"Dad, I think he's figured out how to work the latch—"

"That's clear. I want you to fix it. And when you start those lessons tomorrow, use him. That horse is bored."

Karla Starr gave a between-us-adults chuckle, but Dad ignored her.

Sam thought of Rachel hauling on Ace's tender mouth and knew there was a better way to end his boredom. She needed to take him out and run him. She *was* grounded, but maybe Dad would agree—for Ace's sake.

A raindrop struck her eyelid. Sam blinked. Could those clouds really be ready to give them the rain they needed? A storm would excite Ace. He'd really run for her then.

"I know you all are busy," Karla said, "but I mean what I said. I'd pay top dollar for a horse like your gelding. He's strong enough to carry one rider and pick up a cowboy when his bronc or bull ride is over."

"I'll remember," Dad said, but he was looking skyward and holding back a smile.

Now, while he was pleased, Sam tried to ask.

"Dad, I know if I took Ace out now, I could take the edge off his energy and he'd stay put."

Wind rushed through the cottonwood trees and the horses in the ten-acre pasture began to run.

All at once, there was a tapping sound as rain hit the brim of Dad's Stetson.

Ace tossed his head up, nostrils eager for the rain-sweet air. Then he neighed so loudly Sam covered her ears.

"Please, Dad?"

"Get him tacked up and run him into the wind," Dad said. "But just for a little while."

"Thanks—"

"Don't thank me. Thank your *loco* horse, and take Jake with you." Dad gestured toward the barn where Teddy Bear was tied. "Get after it, and don't be late for dinner. I'm sure Ms. Starr will excuse you."

"Of course." The woman slid her fingers into her pocket and withdrew two business cards. "Sam, people would pay good money to see Ace do what he's getting in trouble for."

Then, looking at Dad, she added, "I don't love my animals, I let them feel useful." Then she handed him the second card. "Just in case you change your mind."

There was something flirty in the gesture that made Sam wish Brynna Olson were there.

Dad nodded politely, and Karla Starr was already driving away when Sam noticed the dog in her truck.

An Australian shepherd stared through the truck's back window. Its one white eye made the dog's stare eerie.

For close to an hour, the dog had stayed silent in the truck cab. If Karla Starr didn't love her animals, how had she trained the dog to be so patient?

Sam didn't want to know.

"C'mon, Ace." She led the gelding by a handful of mane.

Sweetheart was kicking fence rails in the barn corral. Out in the small pasture, Amigo arched his neck and pranced like a stallion ready to do battle. Teddy Bear, tied to the hitching rail, jumped back against his reins as Jake hustled out to plop Sam's saddle into her arms.

"I heard what he said, and this is a fool idea."

"Jake, he'll be fine. Ace always behaves."

Jake ignored her, shaking his head as he frowned after Dad.

"All I can think is that he was so glad you all got

away with all your fingers and toes, he went *loco* himself."

Sam smoothed on Ace's saddle blanket. "What are you trying to say? I don't get it."

"That Karla Starr gives me the creeps," Jake said. "She's after something."

"It's just like you to see a competent businesswoman as a threat," Sam told him, even though she didn't trust Karla Starr, either.

"Competent? Is that what you call it?"

"Sure," Sam said. Without being asked, Ace opened his mouth for the bit.

"And she didn't give you the creeps?"

"Okay, it did bother me when she was sizing up the mustangs as bucking prospects."

"And flashing her business cards around."

"That didn't bother me," Sam said.

"It did," Jake said, "but you won't admit it. I listen to my instincts." Jake pulled Teddy Bear's reins loose from the hitch rail and mounted. "Want to know why?"

"No, but you're going to tell me anyway."

Sam rode beside Jake. By silent agreement, they kept the horses to a walk as they crossed the ranch yard.

"One night, I was trying to get to sleep. I was tossing and turning, feeling like bugs were crawling on me. I knew it was my imagination, 'cause I wasn't camping, just lying in my own bed. Finally one of my brothers — Nate, I think — yelled at me to settle down.

"I did, but I kept feeling like something was trailing on my arm. Really quiet, 'cause I didn't want Nate to beat the tar out of me, I kind of flipped my arm to the side."

Even now, Jake shuddered.

"Something hit the floor. Nate came roaring out of bed and I turned on the light, and there was this ugly black scorpion scuttling across our bedroom floor."

Rain was falling for real now, and Sam pulled up the hood on her slicker.

"You get the point, Brat?" Jake said.

"Yeah, yeah, instincts," Sam muttered.

Jake rode close enough to grab Ace's cheek piece. Because it was Jake, Ace didn't shy, only stopped and flicked his ears in curiosity.

"No, the moral of that story is: if you think something is creeping up to do you harm, don't wait till it fills you with poison."

Chapter Nine ❧

𝓡ain came in sheets, wavering iridescent in the dusk. The sagebrush glowed silver-green as sunset sifted through thunder clouds. The land Sam had known all her life looked alien and exotic.

Jake took the lead, and Sam let Ace follow at a gallop. The wind whipped something past Sam's face. She thought it was a wildflower stalk, until Jake turned to look back over his shoulder. It must have been Jake's leather string, the one he used to tame his long hair, because his black hair looked more like a mane than ever, blowing warrior-wild in the wind.

A white smile showed in his rain-wet face. Thoughts of wild horses made her think Jake shouldn't be confined, either.

Jake liked school and excelled at everything that would make him the good rancher his family wanted him to be, but he wanted to be a police tracker. Sam thought that kind of far-ranging work would suit him best.

A rasping cry sounded overhead and Jake looked up. The hawk had no time for dropping feathers today. Her rounded red tail shifted like a rudder as she sought the safety of her nest.

"Did you send a wish?" Jake shouted, but Sam shook her head. "Hawks carry hopes and prayers to the sky spirits, then bring back blessings. That's what the old ones say."

Jake's words were proof he was feeling as wild as the storm winds. He rarely mentioned his Indian heritage, and Sam knew if she asked him a question now, he'd shrug off the hawk as just part of a story.

The horses galloped through groups of cattle running in sheer joy. With rain spattering their red backs, calves cavorted, holding their tails straight up in the air.

Sam knew she should be afraid to gallop. She wasn't the world's greatest rider, and much of the topsoil had blown away, leaving slippery clay underfoot.

They headed away from the highway and the trail to War Drum Flats. Jake still rode ahead, but now his black hair hung below his Stetson, lying straight and wet to the middle of his back. Teddy's hair was wet, too, and his Bashkir heritage showed in the little C-shaped curls on his rump.

The trail to the canyon was narrow and rough, no place to take a young horse like Teddy.

"Let's turn back," Jake shouted over the hammering rain. His voice was serious.

A single bolt of lightning zigzagged overhead, turning the world aquarium green. Teddy fought for his head, pulling against the reins Jake kept snug.

There wasn't a trace of fun on Jake's face anymore. He concentrated on telling Teddy what to do.

Sam slowed Ace, giving Jake room to work.

Once he had Teddy's attention, Jake forced him to back, to sidestep, anything to remind him his rider was in charge.

Squinting through the rain, Sam saw Teddy begin to relax. Fear drained out of him as he did as he was told. Each time he followed Jake's instructions, Teddy was rewarded. The reins loosened, the bit sat lighter in his mouth, and Jake praised him.

"There you go, partner. Let me do the worryin'," Jake said.

Teddy did, and soon Jake moved him through his gaits with fluid grace, then kept him at a jog.

"That," Sam told Ace, "is the difference between a rider and a horseman. Stick with me a few years and I might be one-tenth that good." She rubbed Ace's neck.

Only after they'd jogged through the rain for five minutes did Jake glance back at Sam.

"Keep your hood up, since you didn't have the sense to wear a hat." He tugged down on his own hat brim, but didn't give her time to argue. "We need to get in before there's more lightning."

Jake let Teddy gallop. Ace followed, lining out

like a racehorse, legs reaching, head level. She trusted Ace to find the best footing. Unlike Teddy, Ace's life had once depended on his instincts.

Still, Sam reminded herself to sit back in the saddle. She was too far forward. If Ace veered or stumbled, she'd fall and Jake would be halfway home before he noticed she was missing. At this pace, they'd cover the five miles to River Bend in no time.

The sky brightened as if lightning was racing above the clouds.

Jake let Teddy out another notch and angled him away from the path home.

It must be because of the lightning. Sam knew you were supposed to stay away from trees, from telephone and power poles, and seek low ground.

That's just what Jake had done, she saw now. He'd steered Teddy into a dry riverbed.

Usually dry. Sam looked around at the low, sandy area. This cloudburst had already turned a few of its dips to puddles. As a child, she'd heard radio broadcasts interrupted by high-pitched signals and an announcer warning against flash floods. She knew that voice had mentioned the dangers of riverbeds.

Ace's run turned choppy, responding to the worry that had tightened Sam's grip on the reins. Starting at her head, working down through her neck, shoulders, and arms, Sam forced her muscles to loosen. Dad had trusted Jake to bring her out here.

"Just follow them," she told Ace. "We'll be fine."

The riverbed narrowed and the banks were nearly as high as the horses' backs.

Dead ahead was a boulder. Sam saw it an instant before Teddy jumped. Too small for the leap, Ace cut through a narrow detour and sprinted ahead. Sam glanced back in time to see Teddy fall.

His jump had been fine. Teddy had cleared the boulder easily, but his front off hoof struck a puddle. Teddy slid, hundreds of pounds of horseflesh sliding on watery mud.

Jake shifted his weight left, trying to give Teddy the help he needed to get centered. Nothing helped.

"Jump!" Sam screamed.

Jake could have, poised to the left as he was, but he stayed with the falling horse. As Teddy's hooves slipped away, his barrel slammed against the right bank. Muscle and bone splattered damp dirt. Teddy grunted, breath knocked from his lungs. Jake's head—tucked in, chin to chest—said he'd been hurt. The fall was smashing his leg between the horse and the riverbank.

Sam pulled Ace to a stop, though she wasn't sure what to do. All four hooves had slid from beneath Teddy. Since Jake had stayed astride, he must be okay. But Teddy's legs thrashed. Was one of those legs broken? Had Teddy ruptured an internal organ or stabbed himself on broken brush? Or was he just struggling to get up?

Only five miles home, she'd thought a minute ago.

Now, five miles seemed an impossibly long distance.

Jake stayed on as Teddy heaved himself up to stand. Jake's hat was gone. He stared down at his saddle horn, and his arms looked boneless, swaying as the horse trembled.

Sam tightened her legs, but Ace didn't want to go closer.

"C'mon, boy, nothing to be afraid of." Sam kept her voice strong. "Teddy needs your company. You're a levelheaded guy. C'mon, Ace."

Thunder grumbled as she reached them, but no lightning flashed. There was just enough light to see rain running down Jake's forehead into his eyes. He did nothing to stop it. A knot of muscle stood out under his skin, showing how hard his jaw was clenched.

"Jake, what hurts?"

It must be everything, she thought, because Jake kept his jaw locked. Or maybe he was afraid that if he opened his mouth he wouldn't be able to stop yelling.

"My horse okay?" he asked, finally.

"Sure. He's up. He's fine." Sam dismissed his question, until she noticed Jake's boot hanging free of his stirrup. "What about your leg?"

"Check him." The effort it cost Jake to say the words made Sam do it.

There was no sense arguing. Jake's concern for himself would wait until he knew Teddy was safe.

Sam turned Ace. They circled Teddy, and though

the cloud-strained evening light made everything look black and white, she could tell he was only a little scuffed.

"A cut on his fetlock and lots of mud. That's it," Sam reported, and then her breath caught.

She saw blood. It was Jake's. A dark patch about the size of her fist had welled through the denim covering his thigh, and it was spreading fast.

"You must have cut your leg when you fell."

She wished Jake would talk. When one corner of his mouth jerked, she thought he was about to laugh, but he only nodded.

"Do you want to stay here while I go get Dad and the truck?"

Jake was shaking his head no before she finished asking.

"Don't be stubborn, Jake. I can tell you're in pain."

He went back to staring at his saddle horn as if it were the most fascinating sight on earth. He took a deep breath, like someone preparing to jump off a cliff, but only uttered a few words.

"Flash flood could come up," he managed. "Or lightning. Don't think—" He looked up at Sam with dark eyes that begged her not to reveal what he was about to say. "Don't think I could handle him."

"Then get down and wait," she demanded.

"Don't think I can do that, either."

Dizziness spun through Sam. Jake was in trouble.

He must have done more than cut his leg. He might have struck his head. He might have some injury he was hiding from her.

Sam didn't know how to assess his injuries, but she knew she was in charge and they were wasting time.

"Okay," she said, but then she felt a flash of pain. If his leg *was* broken, the bone ends would grate as Teddy moved. Jake would be in agony.

"I can ride. Just get my hat," Jake whispered.

Sam slid off Ace, keeping a grip on the reins as she snatched Jake's Stetson from the mud. She brushed it off, only smearing it worse, then handed it up.

Jake didn't notice.

Sam remounted, reined Ace close, and leaned over to put Jake's hat on his wet hair. A wave of tenderness shook her, but Sam refused to let Jake see her distress.

"Typical cowboy," she muttered. "The world could be coming to an end and you wouldn't go outside to watch without your hat."

"You got—" Jake grimaced as Teddy shifted. "Got that right. Now lead us outta here."

Chapter Ten ∾

Jake's trust made Sam careful.

It was up to her to make sure everything turned out all right.

Sam kept Ace at a walk and searched every inch of earth and sky for danger.

Familiar clumps of pine and rock outcroppings passed in slow motion. Though no sensible snake would be out in this downpour, she watched for them. The frolicking Herefords posed no threat. They'd formed into tight, unhappy herds. One group moved toward the ranch, driven by the rain. A few more stood in a miserable cluster, tails clamped down, white eyelashes blinking.

"I guess no one's come looking for us since we're such hotshot range riders," Sam mumbled to Jake. "Why should they worry?"

Jake didn't answer.

Sam rode another few minutes before it struck

her they'd be plenty worried if a horse came home riderless. Sam thought it through. What if she climbed down, gave him a swat, and Ace still didn't leave her?

And Jake wouldn't get off Teddy, even if he could. Pride wouldn't let him lay suffering in the rain until help arrived.

Suddenly Jake was beside her instead of following.

"Faster," he croaked. The bloodstain on his jeans was spreading.

Sam wanted to argue, but his eyes warned her it would be a waste of time.

Sam clapped her heels to Ace, hoping he'd leap straight into a lope. He did, and Teddy imitated him, skipping the hammering trot that Sam knew could finally break Jake's will.

After what seemed like an eternity, a welcome sight appeared on the horizon: smoke, puffing from the chimney at River Bend.

"We're going to make it, Jake."

Sam didn't expect an answer. Only once, when Teddy nearly stumbled, did Jake groan as if the sound had been wrenched from him.

Finally, she let the horses settle to a weary walk.

Just ahead, the bunkhouse windows glowed yellow. All the hands were in from the range, probably eating dinner.

As the horses clopped across the bridge, Sam

thought she saw Gram's face peer from the kitchen window.

Jake held Teddy on a tight rein, refusing to let him pass the front porch for the barn.

As Sam slid from Ace's back, the front door opened and Dad stood there.

"Everything all right?" he asked, looking past her.

"Jake's hurt, Daddy. He's really hurt."

It seemed like Dad reached her in a single stride.

For the first time since that awful sound of bone smashing into the riverbank, Sam let herself cry.

The next afternoon, the baby blue Mercedes was silent. The windshield wipers swished, but no one talked.

Jen stayed quiet, thinking her own thoughts, because that was just Jen. Rachel kept her honey-dew-fuchsia lips pressed together as if she couldn't believe she was sharing the same air with the two lame freshmen. Sam was simply exhausted.

Somehow, she had made it through her morning classes. By lunchtime, though, Sam needed some calories to substitute for sleep. The cafeteria was packed with students wearing new sweaters and jackets it had been too hot to wear until now, and the food lines were disorderly and loud.

All the noise and high spirits reminded Sam of the calves' reaction to the rain. Everyone was glad the drought had broken.

Sam and Jen were balancing their trays and searching for a few feet of table space when Jake's friend Darrell snagged Sam's elbow.

"Hey! I need this hamburger," Sam snapped. And then she recognized Darrell.

He was the kind of guy Gram labeled "bad company," but Sam only knew two things about him. First, he'd taught Jake how to disable a car by pulling loose strategic wires under the hood. Second, Jake didn't want Sam to know him.

Today, defying the rain and school policy, Darrell wore an orange tank top and sunglasses. Where was Mrs. Santos when there was a real delinquent around? Sam wondered.

"What happened to my man Jake?" His index finger hooked the hinge of his sunglasses and pulled them down so he could watch Sam. "I'm hearing bad things."

"What have I missed this time?" Jen despaired.

"I was going to tell you when we found a quiet place," Sam said.

"This looks quiet," Jen said.

It was, because when Jen slammed her tray down next to Darrell's, Jake's usual crew made room with amazement as the girls sat down.

For strength, Sam took a bite of her hamburger, then summed up yesterday's disaster. She had to explain it quickly. If she pictured the fall and that tortured ride, she'd get weepy all over again.

"Jake's horse slipped in the mud and crunched his leg, but Jake insisted on riding back to our place. And so," she finished, "he had a compound fracture—"

"Ahhh man"—Darrell drew the words out in twisted admiration—"like where the busted bone shoves through the skin?"

"Right." Sam nodded.

Her stomach didn't turn over as it had the first time Dad told her what Jake's bloody jeans had hidden. That was progress. And she tried not to recall how they'd made Jake swallow a dose of pain pills and wait for them to take effect before Dallas and Dad moved him from the saddle to the backseat of Gram's Buick.

"And so?" Darrell encouraged her.

"The emergency room doctor put him in a cast and said he'd be down for a while. The Elys were all there by then, so Dad left before they talked about when he could ride."

Darrell made a waving motion as if that didn't matter.

"What about driving?" he asked. "We're supposed to go to Cimmaron for the midnight drag races in a few weeks."

"I don't know. What are drag races?" Sam pictured draft horses pulling heavy loads, but she had a hard time believing Darrell was bereft at the thought of missing such a competition.

"Like with two cars . . . going fast as they can in a

straight line?" Darrell studied Sam for comprehension. "You know."

"Not really," Sam said. She noticed her hamburger was getting cold and began eating again, feeling more ravenous than before.

"When is he coming back to school?" Darrell asked, with no concern at all for her meal.

Sam shrugged and kept eating. She wished the crowd of boys would go away so she could talk to Jen, but it was their table.

Satisfied that they'd leeched the choicest information from her, Darrell and the guys leaned together, talking.

For a minute, Sam wondered if Jake was still in the hospital. She remembered how scared she'd been in a big white hospital bed after her accident two years ago.

She'd been younger, of course, and Jake might not be scared, but he'd hate the limits on his movements. He'd get cranky and restless, though the doctor had said it wasn't an especially bad break.

"So that's where you were when I called last night," Jen said.

"Yeah."

"Your Gram said you were out riding, so I figured you hadn't gotten into trouble." Jen looked at her meaningfully. "You know, over the incident?"

Sam stared at Jen.

"The *school bus* incident?"

"Oh. Yeah." Sam hadn't forgotten really, but the shame she'd felt yesterday had faded. "I'm grounded."

"Even after what you did for Jake?"

Sam considered the question. Her thoughts felt like they were swimming through honey, but she was pretty sure of the answer.

"All I really did was ride along with him, and even if it had been more, well, I can't see one teensy act of heroism erasing what Gram and Dad see as a gigantic mistake."

The end-of-lunch bell rang through the cafeteria. Sam swallowed the last of her soda and stood. "Better go," she said. "Who knows what they'd do to me if I added tardiness to my criminal record."

It was a crummy day to teach Rachel to ride.

When Sam arrived home from school, Gram was in a chatty mood. She announced that Jake had been released from the hospital and was resting in his own bed at Three Ponies Ranch. Of course, Sam couldn't go see him, since Rachel would be arriving soon.

Gram told Sam that Dad and Dallas were on the range, checking the runny-nosed steers. They could have used Sam's help, since Jake was missing from the crew, but they'd ridden out without her because she'd still been at school.

Gram was most excited about her weekend plans. She, Dad, and Brynna were going to the county fair. Gram would compete in the fried chicken cook-off and Dad would meet Brynna's parents.

Sam felt herself staring dully at Gram. She knew it was significant that Brynna wanted to introduce Dad to her parents, but she had no comment. All this information was making her tired. Her eyelids drooped, begging for sleep.

Instead, Sam stood in the drizzle, watching Rachel try to corner Ace and halter him. She felt impatient with them both.

"I don't see why I can't use the pinto one." Rachel stood in the barn corral. Sweetheart crowded up behind her, and Ace was doing everything he could to escape the halter Rachel was pushing at him.

"Because you can't," Sam explained. "And if you expect to get out of there anytime soon, you need to put the lead rope over his neck, like I told you, and reach over the top of his head, like I told you, and slip his nose into that round part. He's not going to do it for you."

Rachel wasn't used to following orders, that was for sure. Even as she did what Sam asked, sort of, she grumbled. "I'd rather ride a 'loud-colored' horse. That's what I read attracts attention to a queen candidate. Ha!"

At last she'd buckled the halter over Ace's head. The glare the gelding gave Sam didn't need words to explain how annoying he found this entire exercise.

"For what I'm paying you," Rachel went on, "the least you can do is have the horse saddled and ready when I get here. And I'd prefer one without a scar on his neck."

A dozen responses hammered through Sam's mind, but she picked the calmest one as she opened the gate.

"This builds the horse's confidence in you, so he'll do what you ask later. Lead him through, Rachel."

Sam figured there was no reason to explain Rachel would never earn the trust of a smart horse like Ace.

"Besides," Sam said as they went to the hitching rail, "I don't think they just present you with a horse—hold the rope with two hands, one closer to his chin—and tell you to do your stuff when you're trying out as a rodeo queen."

"I should find out," Rachel said. "That could save a lot of time. Where's the saddle?"

Sam took the lead rope from Rachel and tied Ace. "In the tack room," she said. "I'll show you."

Sam piled the saddle and blanket on Rachel's arms and slung Ace's bridle over her shoulder.

"I am not a pack animal," Rachel said, her British accent surfacing with scorn.

This is not going to work. Sam gritted her teeth to keep from saying it. Only the tiny possibility that she'd be more patient when she'd had more sleep kept Sam from telling Rachel to go home.

And the fun had just begun.

Ace planted a hoof on the toe of one of Rachel's

new boots. She whimpered.

Ace sidestepped, eyes rolling white. Rachel dropped the saddle.

Ace flung himself to the end of the lead rope, pretending the snaffle was a terrifying foreign object. Rachel recoiled from slimy horse spit.

A long forty minutes later, Ace stood saddled and bridled.

"If you think I'm going to do this every time I come for a lesson, you're delusional," Rachel said as she checked the polish on her fingernails. "I do not like to perspire."

"Could you girls use some cookies and cocoa?" Gram stood on the porch, smiling.

This was what she needed to keep in mind, Sam told herself. Gram cooking happily in the kitchen, the wide ranch house porch, and horses all around. Money made it possible, and that's all she needed from Rachel.

"Let's take a break," Sam said. "Then we'll get you up on Ace."

Sitting on a step, sipping cocoa, Sam stared off toward the ten-acre pasture. Buddy was getting big. Dark Sunshine's pregnancy was beginning to show. Popcorn grazed beside her, looking content.

"Karla Starr is looking for attractive bucking horses," Rachel said.

"I know. She was here just yesterday," Sam said, but she was wondering if the steers with the runny noses had something contagious. She'd ask Dad if Buddy needed an inoculation.

"Sam."

Sam stared. Rachel had never called her that.

"Yes?" Sam watched Rachel watch her. "I heard you. Karla Starr is looking for rough stock. We don't have any."

"I'm just saying . . ." Rachel ran her fingers over the pattern on her cup. She glanced up at Sam, then gave her head a faint shake. "Why should I bother to do you a favor?"

"Rachel, I don't mean to be dense." Sam brushed her bangs away from her eyes. "But I don't know what you're hinting at."

"Karla Starr told my father—oh, this is utter nonsense," Rachel said. "Let's get back to it, shall we?"

By the time Mrs. Coley came for her, Rachel had made some progress in mounting and dismounting from Ace, but Sam had made none in figuring out the clues Rachel had given her.

She trudged toward the house. Maybe Rachel's hints would make sense in the morning. Just now, all Sam knew for sure was that she needed a warm bath, cozy pajamas, and sleep.

Chapter Eleven ∾

Thursday was Jake's birthday.

As Gram drove her over to the Three Ponies Ranch, Sam was not only glad to be getting some time with Jake, she was glad to have a reason for skipping Rachel's lesson.

Only Jen knew how much Sam disliked the after-school chore.

But it wasn't for either of the reasons Jen suspected.

True, Ace acted like a brat-horse around Rachel. He sprinted for the fence rails and tried to rub Rachel off whenever he felt Sam's attention wander. And Rachel was no better. She protested the lack of a covered arena, whining that any civilized ranch needed one for winter. But Ace's tricks and Rachel's stuck-up attitude weren't what made Sam crazy.

Rachel's unending hints were the problem.

She was trying to say something about Karla

Starr, but what? Sam tried to connect Rachel's clues with the fringe from the watering hole and her constant, gnawing worry over the Phantom.

She was hoping that Jake would help her understand. Together, they'd been able to figure out almost anything.

"Welcome to Jake's lair," Mrs. Ely announced as she led Sam to the sunporch where her son sat. "He's cranky as a bear, Sam. We throw him a chunk of raw meat a couple of times a day, but in honor of your visit, I put some iced tea and chips on the table there." Mrs. Ely hesitated. "You're the only one he's agreed to see."

"I'd be flattered," Sam joked as Jake glared past her at his mother, "except that he knows I bought him a cool present back when I got that reward."

As Mrs. Ely and Gram moved off, talking about the county fair and harsh weather, Sam tossed the big, brightly wrapped present toward Jake.

He caught it, but barely, and Sam understood why her friend was so down.

He was embarrassed. His leg was casted straight and jointless. Energetic Jake, who was always bounding off somewhere, couldn't move without help. His jeans were split to go over the white plaster and he wore no shoes.

Had she ever seen Jake's feet before? Bare and pale, they made him look kind of defenseless, so Sam tried not to look. Instead, she took in the wide windows and cascading ferns of the sunporch. And the crutch leaning in one corner.

"Out here, you can pretend it's still summer," she said.

"It's better than my room."

"And you get to skip school."

Jake shook his head and Sam saw how it was. She didn't know how many brothers shared Jake's room, but she could imagine the quiet after they'd all dressed and left him behind.

Sam poured iced tea for both of them. She stared at the slice of bobbing lemon in her glass and resolved to cheer Jake up.

"After you open your present, I have something else for you, too."

Jake's expression said he didn't want to be pitied.

"Open it, Jake. I've been waiting months to see it again." Sam had had the saddle shop wrap the gift in its special packaging. The cardboard was printed to look like hand-tooled leather stamped with the shop's exclusive brand.

"Need some help with that tape and tissue paper, or what?"

"Shut up, Brat," Jake muttered, but then he pushed the wrappings away and stared. He looked up at her, speechless.

"I'm going to put it on Witch for you," Sam said as if she gave hundred-dollar presents every day.

"She'll eat you alive." Jake fingered the split-ear

headstall with something like respect.

"Yeah, and I'm such a good friend, I'll let you watch."

Jake smiled, but it didn't last long.

Sam was glad she'd anticipated this. She'd known that right after he admired the headstall, he'd be sad he couldn't ride with it right away.

"And that's not all." Sam dug into her backpack. "This isn't a present exactly, more like a contribution to your secret ambition."

Jake struggled to sit up straighter. The box and tissue paper slipped away from him before he could grab them.

Pretending she'd intended all along to clear it out of the way, Sam pushed the wrapping aside with one foot and scooted her chair closer to hand him a stack of printouts she'd made from the Internet.

"The Shadow Wolves," she announced in a dramatic voice.

"Thanks." Jake's tone was careful, as if he was trying not to hurt her feelings.

"It's not science fiction or any kind of fantasy, Jake. It's a group of Native American trackers—from several tribes—who help the government catch smugglers. Mostly in the Southwest deserts, but—it's *you*. Take a look."

She'd found the perfect way to end Jake's mope. Once he began reading, he was transformed from sulky to studious.

Outside, the sun ducked behind a cloud. The sun-porch grew dim, but Jake didn't notice. He hardly breathed as he entered the world of men and women whose ancient skills worked better than modern technology to catch criminals sneaking across the desert.

"I didn't know," he muttered, but Sam could tell he wasn't talking to her.

The minute he quit reading, he'd want her gone so he could log on to the Internet looking for details she'd missed.

Sam smiled. It was working out just as she'd hoped. She couldn't give Jake mobility, but she'd given him hours of daydreams.

Somewhere in the ranch house, a window was open. Wind gusted, slamming a door, even as it brought the scent of more rain.

Jake finished reading, then paged back to a photograph illustrating an article.

Gram would want to leave before the roads got too slick. Sam bit her lip. If she was going to ask Jake about the clues, it was now or never.

"I have this situation," she began.

"Figured as much." Jake set the papers aside. "You've been fidgeting for five minutes."

As rain pinged on the aluminum overhang outside, Sam told him everything. His head tilted to one side as he stared out the window.

"You're not stupid, Sam. You just don't want to face facts."

Her heart hammered. She'd counted on Jake to tell her she was just being paranoid.

"Rachel overheard something. She's telling you Karla Starr's after the Phantom."

"But why would she do that? Rachel can't stand me."

"Don't ask me to look into her head. I don't want to be there." He pretended to shudder. "But the horses, now . . ."

Jake's eyes lost focus as he sank deeper into the chair.

"The key to how she's catching horses is in the way Silly and Ace reacted at the water hole. They're domesticated. A trap shouldn't scare them." He rocked forward and his fist struck the table in frustration. "If I could get out there and look around—"

"You wouldn't find a darn thing, because it's been raining for days. So forget that."

"Don't get uppity or I'll hit you with my crutch."

"You will not." Sam didn't feel like joking. She warmed her arms against a chill that had nothing to do with the rain. How could she help the Phantom?

"Tell Brynna." Jake turned one hand palm up, as if the solution to Sam's worry was obvious. "If I could ride, I'd go check it out with you. That terrain's too rough for you alone, but she can send a ranger or wrangler up to the high country to look for him. It'd be best, you know, if you told them exactly where to find him. There's nothing else you can do."

Jake was wrong. She could ride Ace to the Phantom's hidden valley. He might even come to her. Being grounded would make it tougher, but Gram and Dad were going to the county fair. They expected her to go along, but maybe she wouldn't.

"I can see the wheels turnin', but with that river rising, it's too dangerous to risk going alone. Don't cross your arms and get all huffy with me. I didn't do no rain dance."

Jake was trying to tease her. He knew he couldn't stop her himself, and he didn't want to tell on her. But he would. He'd done it before.

Sam heard footsteps approaching. She stood to go, feeling more irritated and confused than when she'd arrived.

Jake grabbed her sleeve and his voice turned gruff.

"Get it through your thick head, Sam. Rodeo season's nearly over. If Karla Starr wants the Phantom, she probably already has him."

When she got home and jogged into the barn, Sam expected to see Ace waiting impatiently for her.

Instead, she saw Brynna Olson kissing Dad right on the lips.

Sam froze. As far as she knew, they'd only been on one date. She had caught Dad talking on the phone to Brynna a couple of times, but still . . .

They were in the barn, just outside the tack room.

Even though Brynna wore her red hair in a tight braid and her BLM uniform, she looked anything but professional. And though Dad's hands rested on each of her shoulders, he was not pushing her away.

And then they noticed her.

Dad had the decency to look embarrassed. Brynna blushed, then giggled. "We didn't hear you."

"No kidding?" Sam itched to inform Brynna a thirty-something woman shouldn't giggle. But she couldn't do it.

She liked Brynna in most ways, and Dad's expression warned Sam that her tone had come close to crossing the line.

Since no one seemed to know what to say, Sam turned to Ace.

His head hung over the fence facing into the barn. He tossed his forelock, showing off the white star between his eyes.

Sam stood close and let him nuzzle her neck. She closed her eyes, and though she heard Dad and Brynna talking about the county fair and Brynna's parents' coming to meet Dad, she was thinking of the Phantom.

Sure, she was mad at Brynna, but Brynna cared about her job. And her job was to protect Nevada's wild horses.

"I think Karla Starr is trapping wild horses," Sam said loudly.

Dad's eyes narrowed.

Brynna turned, took in his expression, then faced Sam. "Who's Karla Starr?"

"She's a rodeo contractor—" Sam started.

"Strictly small-time," Dad interrupted, but Brynna was still listening to Sam.

"She's said things that sort of sound like she doesn't think the law applies to her." Sam hadn't put the thought in words before, but she felt it was the truth. Like Slocum, Karla Starr thought she could make herself an exception to the rules.

"Anything else?" Brynna looked willing to be convinced.

"Rachel Slocum has been hinting that her father told Karla Starr about the Phantom to 'sweeten the deal' he was making to sell her some of his Brahma bulls."

Brynna nodded, encouraging her. "What else?"

"Isn't that enough?" Sam demanded, as Brynna looked at Dad.

"Wyatt?"

"I don't know why she'd do that if she wanted to stay in business."

"And out of jail." Brynna was actually smiling.

"Because she thinks she can get away with it!" Sam snapped.

Karla Starr *would* get away with it, too, if Dad and Brynna didn't pay attention instead of making goo-goo eyes at each other.

"What exactly did Rachel say?" Brynna asked.

"Just a bunch of stuff." Sam's frustration swelled as Brynna glanced at Dad again. "I didn't write it down, okay?"

"Okay," Brynna agreed. "Sam, you were right about Slocum before, and I trust your judgment. You want what's best for the horses and so do I. I'll tell the rangers to keep an eye out for any unusual activity—"

"I have her business card," Sam said, but Dad had already taken his copy of the card from his wallet.

Brynna studied the card. "We'll check her out."

"You can have someone keep watch on the Phantom, too, can't you?"

"I wish I could, but I only have two men to patrol ten thousand acres." Brynna's weight shifted toward Dad.

It must have been some kind of cue.

"Friday night we're driving in for the fair," Dad said. "We figured you'd want to come along and watch your Gram win a blue ribbon for her fried chicken."

We figured. Sam ran the sentence over in her mind. Dad and Brynna. Together. Overnight. They'd be with Gram, but it still sounded awfully serious.

"Maybe," Sam said. "I have a history project I need to work on, though."

Sam waited for Dad to tell her she didn't have a choice. After all, it was pretty clear he was going. And not to watch Gram, either.

She looked him straight in the eyes. Arms crossed,

he mirrored her own stubborn stance. But he'd never left her alone overnight. Would he do it now?

"Suit yourself," Dad said.

"I will." Sam gave Ace a pat and started out of the barn.

She couldn't believe this. How was she supposed to feel?

They were watching her. Every step seemed to take forever. She'd longed for Dad to trust her enough to leave her alone overnight, but now he was doing it for all the wrong reasons.

"She'll get over it," Brynna whispered.

And though the angel on Sam's shoulder was assuring her that Brynna meant it in the nicest way possible, her little horned conscience was saying, "That settles it. I'm doing this my own way."

Chapter Twelve ∾

The wind shrieked so loudly, rushing around the ranch house all night, not even Blaze heard the hens squawking when half their house was smashed to splinters beneath the cottonwood tree.

Sometime after midnight, a combination of drought, rain, and wind had forced the tree to tip over. When Gram and Sam walked out to hurry through morning chores before Gram left for the fair and Sam for school, the cottonwood tree was tilted, branches down, roots up.

"Oh, my goodness!" Gram's hand covered her lips, but only for an instant. "Help me count them, Samantha."

Since there was nothing to be done about the tree, Sam did as Gram asked, counting the Rhode Island red hens who had hopped over the flattened fence.

"At least they were smart enough to stick around," Sam said, and when they'd both counted twice, it turned out she was right.

Three hens had been trapped inside, unharmed, and the rest had decided freedom wasn't worth drowning for. They huddled clucking and complaining near their house, waiting for Gram to do something.

Would Gram stay home after all?

Sam looked at the tree roots, skeletal and black against the gray sky. Was this a sign that she shouldn't ride out to check the Phantom even if Gram and Dad were gone?

"Well, ain't that an awful-looking thing?" Dallas had come from the bunkhouse. Hatless and smelling of maple syrup, he stood with his hands on his hips. "The other boys are still eating, but we can get this put together in no time."

"I don't know," Gram fretted.

"Don't even think about skipping your trip," Dallas scolded. "All we was going to do today was push those heifers back uphill again. Seems they remember grazin' down here when winter's coming on, so they want to stay down, no matter if higher ground is safer with all this rain.

"You and Wyatt go on. Nothing here the rest of us can't take care of. Isn't that right, Samantha?"

Sam swallowed hard and nodded.

Dallas's question and her own uneasiness kept Sam in a haze of guilt all day. Gram had kissed her good-bye, promising to call both Friday and Saturday nights. Dad had told her to let Dallas and the hands worry about the chores. All she had to do was study and enjoy having the house to herself until they got home Sunday evening. When he'd given her a hug that lifted her off her feet, Sam almost cried.

As the school day passed, evidence kept piling up to convince Sam she'd make a lousy criminal.

She was gathering her book and notebook at the end of history class when Mrs. Ely asked what she had planned for the weekend. Sam panicked.

"Why? What do you mean?"

"I just thought you might come over and keep Jake company." Mrs. Ely looked up from her gradebook, eyebrows raised.

"I'm working on my history project." Sam fell back on her cover story without thinking that Mrs. Ely was the one who'd made the assignment.

"Oh. Good." She looked surprised. "How great that you're getting an early start."

At lunch, Jen asked the same question.

"Why do you want to know?" Sam demanded.

"Don't jump down my throat. I was just going to see if you wanted to come over for popcorn and videos, since your dad and Gram are going to be gone."

"How did you know?"

"You told me," Jen said patiently. "And you talked about it with Mrs. Coley this morning in the car, remember? Because she's going to the fair, too, and my mom's picking us up?"

"Oh. Yeah. No, I can't come over. I'm working on my history project."

"Fine." Jen held her palms out as if her agitated friend might charge. "I guess you're trying to get off restriction early by getting good grades."

The bell rang.

"Right," Sam agreed, but as she walked to class, Sam decided there was another reason to get good grades. If she flunked out of high school and turned to a life of crime, she'd be down at the police station confessing before she did one thing wrong.

Sam had never really considered Jen's mom, Lila Kenworthy. If she noticed anything about her, it was her faint Texas accent and her tendency to look tired. But not today.

When Lila pulled up in the Darton High parking lot, driving the Mercedes in place of Mrs. Coley, even Jen noticed the difference.

Jen slid into the backseat first, and Sam heard her ask, "Are you—are we going somewhere, Mom?"

"Jen." Mrs. Kenworthy's voice held a gentle reprimand.

"Thanks for picking us up," Sam said. She noticed Mrs. Kenworthy's short blond hair was poufy and she wore eye makeup.

"No problem," she said, but her attention seemed focused on Rachel.

Rachel entered the car wordlessly. She wore jeans, a white top, and a canary yellow overblouse that kept the outfit from looking casual. She fastened her seat belt, then waited a few seconds to see if someone would trot around and close the door for her. When no one did, she sighed, leaned out, and pulled it closed herself. But she didn't say a word to Jen's mother.

"Did Dad get Maniac loaded all right?" Jen asked, then added for Sam's benefit, "He's entered in the best-of-breed competition at the fair."

Sam guessed that was another difference between Linc Slocum and Dad. If Dad wanted to show an animal in the county fair, he loaded it into a trailer and drove it there himself.

"They came to an agreement after a while," her mother said.

Sam didn't envy Jed Kenworthy the task of convincing the tiger-faced Brahma bull to enter a stock truck.

They were on the highway, headed for home, when Jen's mom spoke again. "So, Rachel, I hear you want to be a rodeo queen."

Sam had expected Jen to keep Rachel's secret. Judging by Jen's open mouth and wide eyes, she'd hoped her mom would keep it, too.

Rachel straightened with the grace of a Siamese cat and gave Jen a look such as a cat might give a mouse, but her voice sounded polite.

"Why yes, Mrs. Kenworthy, that's so. I've been

toying with the idea, although I'm discovering it's not as easy as it looks. Jen tells me you competed."

"I did, and that's why I brought it up. I'd be glad to help if I can."

Jen stared at the back of her mother's head as if she'd begun speaking Swahili. From what Jen had said before, Sam knew the Kenworthys and Rachel exchanged fewer than a dozen words each month.

"I do have one advisor who's competed more recently." Rachel blinked in a leisurely manner that showed off her eyelashes. "However, I'd appreciate your impressions. Especially what you learned from the experience."

Sam had never seen Rachel's charm in action. She knew some people—even teachers, who should be wiser—liked Rachel, but since the rich girl had never tried to impress her, Sam hadn't seen this side of her.

"What did I learn?" Mrs. Kenworthy relaxed into the driver's seat. When she talked next, there was a smile in her voice. "I learned to put on mascara in a moving truck. I learned to go to school in hand-me-down clothes because anything I bought new had to have sequins. I learned to make a loop of duct tape, stick it to my forehead, and press my hat against it so it didn't blow off as I galloped around the arena.

"You'll lose points for that, you know, when you're being judged," Mrs. Kenworthy's dancing eyes rose to the rearview mirror. "Girls these days can use double-sided tape."

"Double-sided tape," Rachel repeated, touching her forehead. "But doesn't that irritate your skin?"

"It leaves a red line, but nobody'll see it except your horse, because you're never without your hat."

Jen seemed to be studying her mother, weighing her words. Sam wondered if the woman was trying to discourage Rachel or just give her a reality check.

As they passed War Drum Flats, Sam looked out the window for mustangs. The entire area was a different color than usual, darkened by days of rain, but there wasn't a horse in sight. Lila Kenworthy drove in silence for a few miles, and Sam saw only a few cattle searching for grass.

"Honestly, though, Rachel," Jen's mom continued, "the two big things I learned were to ride any horse they pushed at me—sometimes you'll ride one belonging to the stock contractor, you know, and not your own—and to get along with people."

"Now, that's a valuable skill." Jen seemed set on interrupting her mother's lecture.

It almost worked.

With the River Bend bridge in sight, Mrs. Kenworthy added, "At least your dad won't have to take out a loan on your house to pay for cases of hair spray. My dad was always joking about that."

The horses had congregated on the far end of the ten-acre pasture and made no move to greet Sam. Beneath overcast skies, the ranch yard stood gray and empty.

The cottonwood tree had vanished, and the ranch hands had done such a good job of repairing the hen house and fence, Sam had to look carefully to see where they'd patched and nailed.

When she started up to the house, Sam smelled the fresh-sawed wood. The tree had been cut into lengths for the fireplace and stacked neatly on the front porch to dry.

Sam shrugged off her backpack, but before she went into the empty house, she checked on Ace. Only a few days had passed between her decision to ride into the Phantom's canyon alone and now. She hadn't been able to give Ace the endurance preparation he deserved for such a long, hard ride.

"I'm counting on your mustang toughness," Sam told Ace when she reached the barn. Ace shoved his chest against the fence. "No, you rest."

"What for?" Dallas shuffled into the barn.

Sam let out a squeak of surprise.

"Sorry, didn't mean to startle you, hon," he said. "Guess you and Ace were having a personal conversation."

When he patted the gelding's neck, Sam noticed Dallas's knuckles were swollen. And yet Dad had given him and the other hands her weekend chores so she could "study."

"Why don't you quit work early, today, Dal?"

"Been doin' that all week. This rain's like a vacation, 'cept for resetting fence posts that are washing out of where they're set." Dallas shook his head.

"This ground's soaked up about all the water it can hold. You be careful if you go out riding early."

Sam smiled, but she felt a little sick. Dallas himself had supplied an excuse for her absence. Hadn't Dad told him she was grounded?

Straw rustled in a stall that was usually empty. As Sam moved to look inside, Dallas explained.

"It's Buddy. Thought you might like to help me give her that inoculation. Just a precaution, but your Dad likes to be careful with her."

"Sure," Sam said. In fact, she didn't want to help give Buddy a shot, but Buddy would appreciate her nearness.

When Dallas came with the syringe, Sam wrapped her arms around Buddy's furry red body.

"It'll just take a minute," she crooned to the calf as Dallas held up the syringe and flicked it. "Just a minute, and you get to stay in this nice warm stall."

Buddy gave a surprised bleat, and her ears flapped, but that was all. She twisted to get free and Sam released her.

"No problem," Dallas said. "Guess your bulldoggin' career is over."

Reminded of rodeos and Karla Starr, Sam took a breath. Dallas had worked for a stock contractor. That made him an expert. She had to ask.

"Dal, there's talk . . ."

"There always is." The foreman's gray-haired head came up as he said it, though, and his expression turned attentive.

"Do you think it's possible Karla Starr would catch mustangs to use as bucking horses?"

"Possible? Sure. And that gray stud you like would be a prize. He'd be a real crowd pleaser 'cause he's pretty, and a real arm-jerker 'cause he's strong. A cowboy could earn a lot of points if he stayed on. And if he didn't—well, that's every rodeo fan's fantasy, to see a horse that's never been rode."

Sam's spirits fell lower than ever, until Dallas crossed his arms as he leaned against Ace's corral. "Now, is that likely? Not if she's just starting out and wants to stay in business. There's ways to catch mustangs, of course, but to my way of thinking, it's just not worth the risk."

"That's what Brynna Olson thinks, too. And Dad."

Sam relaxed, feeling like she'd just climbed into a warm bathtub. Obviously, Karla Starr wouldn't do such a thing. The Phantom was probably holed up in his cozy canyon with his mares and foals, waiting out the storms.

Sam might have given up her whole plan if Dallas hadn't started nodding and added, "Then again, some folks think they can get away with anything and not get caught. Heck, sometimes they're right."

Sam paced. If she was going to go, she should go tonight, right after Gram called, so she'd be back by the time Gram called again Saturday night.

She warmed up the dinner Gram had left for her. When she realized it was only four o'clock, Sam left the meal on the counter, ate three cookies, and drank some milk.

This was stupid. It wasn't raining now, but it was wet, and she'd seen Teddy go down in slippery footing. She shouldn't endanger Ace. Or herself.

She unloaded her backpack onto her bed, then scurried around the house. She gathered a flashlight, matches, granola bars, and an apple, and put everything in plastic bags inside her backpack.

Would it be safer to ride out tonight or leave before daylight tomorrow? She couldn't decide.

Then, Sam remembered telling Dad she wasn't like Rachel, who'd snatched Champ and sneaked away. Sam dumped the supplies out of her backpack. She was *not* going.

Without reheating it, Sam ate the meat loaf and mashed potatoes Gram had left. She ate standing, staring at the kitchen clock, and remembered the Phantom in the BLM corrals. Mane tangled, eyes crazy with fear, he'd slammed himself bloody against the fence rails. How much worse would he feel after being trucked from rodeo to rodeo, when men tried to ride him? Would he remember how she'd led him gently to the river and climbed on his back long ago? Would he blame her somehow?

Sam ran down to the barn and grabbed a slicker. It was dusk and the smell of spaghetti sauce came from the bunkhouse kitchen. The hands were having dinner, so they hadn't seen her. Probably. But why had she brought the slicker to the house? She should have left it in the barn, near Ace, so she could wear it when she rode out. If she rode out.

By the time Gram called, Sam had changed her mind a dozen more times. Gram asked if she'd eaten. Sam rinsed her dish as she told Gram the meat loaf was great. As Gram told how they'd stopped for lunch in Darton, how they were meeting Brynna Olson's parents for dinner at a steak house, Sam wanted to scream with tension.

"The first round of the chicken cook-off is at nine tomorrow morning—Samantha, is everything all right?"

Sam looked at the telephone receiver. She didn't know what to say. "Everything's fine. I miss you guys."

"Well, we miss you, too. I'll call you tomorrow night and tell you what we won. Good night, sweetie."

It was the right thing to say, because Gram hung up happy.

Sam walked out to the front porch and faced into a warm breeze. She heard a night bird's call, but not a single splat of rain dripping from the eaves. Dark and light flickered inside the bunkhouse, where the hands were watching television.

Sam stared into the night sky. She could see stars, not clouds. Maybe the storms had gone east. Maybe the wind and rain wouldn't return for weeks. If she left tonight, she'd have plenty of time. She wouldn't rush or make mistakes.

In ten minutes, she'd pulled on her boots, hat, slicker, and backpack full of supplies. She left a few strategic lights and the television on, and started toward the barn.

Ace's neigh floated through the night, urging her to hurry, and Sam felt better. Ace wanted to go.

By daybreak, they'd both be in the canyon. Ace would be home, and she would be relieved, watching sunbeams turn Zanzibar's coat to silky silver.

Chapter Thirteen ↷

Ace knew he was going back to his first home. He loped through starlight, head high, breathing the fragrance of sagebrush and creosote bush. A few hours without rain had improved the footing. His hooves struck the dirt in a smooth rhythm as he swooped to miss puddles.

They headed toward War Drum Flats, cut left through a brushy ravine, and traveled up through a series of switchbacks. Ace negotiated the zigzags with such precision, Sam felt light-headed by the time they reached the boulder that nearly blocked the tunnel to the valley.

They slipped past it, and Ace's hooves echoed on the rock floor. Sam pressed her cheek against his neck, staying low to avoid hitting her head on the stone ceiling. Along here, somewhere, cracks crossed the ceiling. She'd seen light shine through them before, sparkling on the Phantom's coat.

Tonight there was only darkness.

"Whoa. Ace, ow! That was my head. *Whoa*. I'm getting off."

The gelding danced in eagerness, so Sam kept a grip on the reins as she climbed down. She heard far-away sounds that could be questioning nickers or water running over rocks.

The Phantom had always greeted them before. Ace had bowed to the stallion's authority and followed at his kingly pace. This time, Ace's hooves clipped her boot heels and he shoved her along with his chest.

"No!" She turned to face him, but could barely see his outline. He filled the gloom as he tried to shoulder past.

"Ace, you're only here for a visit." Sam gave a light tug on the reins, reminding him he wasn't returning to the wild.

The gelding blew through his lips and followed Sam.

She saw stone walls soar against black sky strewn with a million diamond stars. She saw shadowy horses, alert at this invasion, and then the stallion trumpeted a challenge and charged.

He wasn't the Phantom.

In the instant before she clamored atop a boulder, pulling Ace out of harm's way, Sam knew it was a different horse. This stallion was taller, darker, younger.

"Hey!" she shouted.

The horse veered, unnerved by her human voice.

Sam squinted, wishing she could see more than a murky shape, but as she huddled against the boulders, waiting for the light, it was enough to know the Phantom was gone.

Sam stared at her glowing watch dial, trying to guess when it would be light enough to see the entire herd and know for sure the Phantom wasn't there.

She knew the charging stallion hadn't been him, but what if the horse had defeated the Phantom and left him injured?

Sam rubbed her cheeks to keep them warm. Rain was pelting down again. She sat under a shelf of rock as she made a plan.

If the Phantom wasn't there, Karla Starr probably had him. Sam tried to accept that fact without imagining details. Her job was to hurry home, phone the number Gram had given her for their motel, and put Brynna on Karla Starr's trail.

If that failed, she'd call the telephone number on Karla Starr's business card and find out which rodeo—if any—the woman had supplied stock for this weekend.

"And then—" Sam saw Ace look her way.

Intimidated by the new stallion, the gelding had stayed nearby, even after Sam turned him loose.

"—I'll get Dallas to drive me to her ranch, or the rodeo, and I'll get the Phantom myself."

At last morning was brightening the sky, and

though her horsewoman's heart rejoiced at the beautiful animals before her, Sam closed her eyes.

He wasn't there. Sleek and wet, dozens of horses moved through the grass with their foals. Brown, red, gray, and tan coats shone darker from days of rain. The tiger dun mare stood guard, watching the new stallion. Her caution said she didn't trust him completely, and Sam realized why.

He was one of the bachelors, the young black horse that Mrs. Coley had called New Moon. A son of the Phantom, he'd returned to the herd and discovered his father gone. Without a fight, he'd taken over.

Sam tacked up Ace and hurried toward the tunnel. Before she left the enchanted valley, she looked back.

"Don't get too comfy, Moon. I'm coming back, and when I do, I'm bringing your dad."

Going back through the tunnel was even scarier than usual. Sam imagined the tons of rocks overhead. An earthquake could bring them crashing down or an avalanche could sweep the entire tunnel off the mountain's face.

When she reached the mouth of the tunnel, she couldn't believe the water. It was like facing a waterfall.

Sam looked back into the tunnel. Should she stay until the downpour slacked off or risk Ace's legs on the shale-shingled mountainside?

If Dallas had come over to the house, he'd see the lights she'd left on and hear the television. If she didn't answer his knock at the door, he might think she was sleeping. Or he'd notice Ace gone and know she'd ridden out.

"What do you think, Ace?" Sam stood next to him, arm slung around his neck. His body warmed her, even through the slicker. "You know the desert better than I do. I sure wish you could talk."

Since he couldn't, Sam swung into the saddle and tried to read each movement. His ears pricked forward, seeming eager to go, and he moved out. For a few steps his head lowered, trying to escape the pelting rain. When he found that impossible, he ignored it, picking his way down the hillside on a path only he could see. Somehow, he seemed to miss most of the plate-size disks of slate that could slide them in directions they didn't want to go.

Far below, she saw the river. It looked wrong. Not placid and blue-green, but squirming across the range like a chocolate-brown anaconda.

Sam looked away.

About halfway down, Ace couldn't sidestep the storm's damage. Water had run in the mustang trails, making them into channels, then overflowed, branching into many-fingered streams and connecting the paths. Lower down, water had cut through shelves of dirt and crumbled them off in chunks.

They were almost down when the trail began collapsing at the touch of Ace's hooves. Just ahead lay War Drum Flats, but it didn't look right. The water hole was filled. It had overflowed its banks and washed out the dirt road leading down from the highway.

"Back up," Sam told Ace. "We'll just have to forget about the path. We'll go along the hillside and look down for a place that's not too steep."

When they crashed through the brushy ravine where mustangs hid, they found it full of cattle. Ace tossed his head up, and balked, but the white-faced animals didn't spook. In fact, when Sam reined Ace aside, they followed him.

If he hadn't been so tired, Ace would have resisted as more lowing cattle and their calves fell in around them. He snorted, knowing he should be chasing them, not the other way around.

Sam understood. Riders not only herded the cattle to better pastures, they'd brought the Herefords out of dangerous situations before. These cattle were insisting—in loud, bawling voices—that she should get busy helping them, now.

One heifer with a face splotched brown and white made a panicky sound like a cuckoo clock.

Ace pinned his ears and lunged at her, teeth bared, before Sam could rein him around.

"*Whoa*, darn it! We've got bigger trouble than her. Aren't we right across the river from the ranch, Ace? Where is it?"

Sam stared into the rain, which had softened into a wet fog. She couldn't see the bridge or the lights she'd left on upstairs or a place to cross. The flood had washed away landmarks. The one willow tree she thought she recognized had stood on the wild side of the river. Now it stood at midstream.

There. At last she saw the house and barn. They were on higher ground. If she could just get the cows and calves across the river, they'd be safe—if crowded—in the pens.

And it looked like there might be a place to cross. Sam tried to understand what her eyes saw. Just upstream from where the bridge should be was a spit of land. It was shaped sort of like a cooking spoon, except with handles on both sides. And the farthest one—the bridge of ground leading home—was skinny.

As they rode closer, Sam was amazed. The water was so churned up it really looked like cocoa covered with foam. Uprooted sagebrush rode the waves. A board, painted yellow and hinged, hit a submerged rock and launched into the air.

Sam pulled Ace back a step. His hooves splashed. Water was everywhere.

Suddenly, the brackle-faced heifer dashed past. Ace was still gathering himself when the cow belly flopped into the river.

Sam jerked Ace around, using his brown body to keep the other cattle from following. She flapped her hat toward the eye-rolling white faces. They didn't follow, only looked after the heifer. She wasn't swimming. She was being swept downstream by a surge of muddy water.

"Poor silly thing." Sam blinked then, suddenly aware of what she was seeing.

She was a rancher's daughter, and the ranch was already in trouble. One heifer lost was a heifer who wouldn't calve, who wouldn't go to market, who was a loss the River Bend could not afford.

All week Dal and the hands had herded cattle to higher ground. But this contrary bunch had returned to the riverfront pasture.

Now, no matter how much she wanted to get back home, it was Sam's turn to herd. For the animals' own good, she must scare the heck out of them and hope they ran for the mountains.

Sam loosed the rope on her saddle and shook out a loop. She had no intention of lassoing a single cow. She couldn't, with all her shivering. But the cows didn't have to know that.

Sam whooped. She flashed the rope at the cows' pink noses.

"Git, git, git!" she shrieked.

The cattle understood exactly what this meant, and so did Ace.

"Go on, cows!" Sam yipped like a coyote and snapped the rope at furry red haunches.

The cattle crowded away, rolling their eyes and

making short, hooting bellows.

Ace grunted, shoving the cattle before him while Sam wielded the rope like a bullwhip.

They bolted and ran. One calf slipped, righted herself, and crashed into her mother in her rush to escape the wailing human on her heels.

Ace chased the herd until they were running toward the Calico Mountains.

I should follow them. That would be the safest move. But even as Sam thought it, she was pulling Ace into a wide turn back toward the river.

If Pepper, Ross, and Dallas thought she was in danger, they'd come after her. For their safety, if not to stay out of more trouble, she must try to cross that spoon-shaped spit of land.

She wasn't the only one with that idea.

Dead ahead were more cows. While her back had been turned, a handful of cattle had tried the same thing, then stopped.

"We'll take them home," Sam told Ace. "B-B-Buddy will enjoy the company."

Not only was she shivering, her head hurt as if she were getting sick, and icy rain sluiced down her neck. She should put her hood up under her hat, but her hands were so numbed with cold, she was afraid she'd drop her hat.

What was that sound? As Ace poised to step on the land bridge, Sam thought the bumpy brown earth looked like the spine of a sunken dinosaur. And that grinding sounded like something with stone teeth. . . .

Stop it, Sam told herself. She clucked to Ace and he walked calmly toward the milling cattle crowded on the little hilltop that had turned into an island.

Then Sam saw the source of the sound. There was no dinosaur in the river, but the truth was almost as bad. The mighty current had scoured the range and swept everything along. Now it was bouncing boulders along like basketballs.

The River Bend bridge was close; it had never looked more welcoming.

"Let's go home, Ace," Sam said.

As the gelding moved, two Herefords rushed away from him. Clumsy from fear, they hurried side by side along the dirt tightrope to shore. It crumbled beneath them.

With the instincts of a great cow pony, Ace tried to go after them. Sam yanked her reins tight. No way in the world would she risk him, no matter the cost.

A whirlpool spun the heifers until they couldn't tell which direction to swim. Sam was glad the foggy rain hid them from her before she had to watch them drown.

She and Ace must weigh less than the two summer-fat Herefords, but should she risk it or go back? Sam looked over her shoulder. The way back was twice as long, and fingers of muddy water were spreading across it.

She could stay where she was with seven panicky Herefords and her horse. If she stayed, she might still be there when the water covered the little island completely.

Sam leaned forward and hugged Ace hard. She had to decide for both of them.

And for the Phantom. If something happened to her, the BLM might not know he'd disappeared for years.

They had to go on and hope the cattle didn't try to follow. Once she got across, she'd try to rope each cow and pull it to shore.

"We can do this, Ace." Sam gathered her reins and analyzed the path leading home.

About as wide as her rib cage and two car lengths long, it wouldn't challenge Ace at all if it weren't for the roaring river and forlorn cows.

"We'll be back for you, ladies." Sam hoped it was true.

She balanced in the saddle, trying to make her position perfect for Ace. "Step lightly, boy."

Before Sam gave Ace the cue to move, a voice came through the stormy commotion.

"Samantha!"

She knew the voice, but she couldn't see the speaker.

"Stay put for a second. I'll toss you a loop and you'll knot it around your waist."

A shadowy horse and rider took shape on the bridge.

"Tie it right. You know how. Then put Ace to that

little dirt trail. He's a good pony. But if he falls, I'll pull you to shore."

It was Dallas. He sounded young and sure. Sam brushed aside thoughts of his stiff walk, his arthritis, and bad back. She hoped he felt as competent as he sounded. Her life might depend upon it.

Chapter Fourteen ⌾

A lariat sang out of the mist and hit Sam's shoulder. She grabbed the riata before it could fall.

Dallas's braided rawhide rope felt almost alive in Sam's hands. She flexed her cold fingers before passing the rope around her waist, then tied the same knot she used to hitch Ace. No doubt there was a better knot for this job, but she didn't know it, and there was no time for Dallas to shout instructions.

Sam jerked on the riata. The knot held.

She waved her arm to tell Dallas she was coming over, then smooched at Ace to go ahead.

The rain had slacked off, but the wind had picked up. It blew Ace's forelock straight back, out of his eyes.

Good, Sam thought, *we need all the help we can get.*

Sam kept her eyes fixed on the opposite shore. Jake had always told her a rider should look where she wanted to go. It was important to do things right.

So, though Sam worried about the cattle shuffling behind her, she looked ahead.

A windblown wave gobbled the last few yards of the path. As it turned to dirt, then slurry, then liquid, Ace leaped.

Hind legs thrust them forward. Front legs straightened and reached. They touched, but his body was too short. As Ace's forelegs scrabbled on shore, his hind legs slipped.

The riata tightened. Sam's legs and Ace's hindquarters plunged into a cold tide that yanked and tugged, determined to wash them downstream.

Ace's neck whipped forward, straining to bring the rest of his body along. It didn't help. The mustang refused to give up, but his loud panting said he was exhausted.

Sam felt Dallas's riata tighten yet again. The foreman was giving Ace one last try before jerking Sam free. It would save Sam, but the sudden imbalance would surely send Ace spinning down the river.

Ace's hind legs kicked. Sam felt his haunches dropping, hooves seeking earth to brace against. He found nothing but fast-moving water.

The riata closed hard on Sam's ribs. She grabbed onto the saddle horn. She would not leave her horse.

"Come on, boy. You can do it, Ace."

With a mighty heave of shoulder muscle, Ace rose and hurled his body forward. Something sang in the air and Ace slid forward on his belly. Snakelike, he was gliding on the muddy riverbank, closer to the bridge.

And then he stopped, beyond the reach of the flood-frenzied river.

Confused and breathless, Sam rolled free of Ace. She worked the riata over her head before turning to see Ace boost himself to all four hooves and shake like a giant, wet dog.

Dallas rode toward them, slowly gathering the slack from a second rope.

"Easy, horse, that's it." Dallas clucked as he rode closer. The other end of the rope he was coiling had caught Ace just behind the forelegs, around the barrel. "Surprised that worked." Dallas chuckled. "If he hadn't reared up that way, I'd've laid the loop over his neck, but . . ."

Sam knew what he didn't want to say. With the river pulling one way and Dallas the other, Ace might have strangled.

Black dots swarmed over Sam's field of vision. Her knees unlatched and her legs wobbled.

"Sam!" Dallas shouted. "Stay with me, girl."

She straightened and stared at him. Dallas's blue eyes were the only color in the gloomy day.

"Take this knife." He extended it toward her. "Open it, and cut that rope."

Sam took the knife and staggered toward Ace. She would have steadied herself against him, but Ace pinned his ears back, warning her away.

"Just cut it, Samantha. That pony's had enough aggravation."

Sam sawed at the rope. A few strands twisted loose.

"Don't give up on hacking that," Dallas said. "If you reach down and try to take that loop off, he might just decide to give your head a kick for getting him into this mess."

Finally freed, Ace trotted toward the barn. He glanced back only once, shaking his ears at Sam as if he'd understood Dallas's idea and liked it just fine.

"Dallas, I'm sorry." Sam's words came out on a shaky breath.

"Wait." Dallas urged Amigo toward the raging water, though the old horse was shaking from the exertion of pulling Ace and Sam up the bank.

Milling and mooing, the cattle were wondering what to do. Dallas frightened them into action.

"One more time, old friend." Dallas spun his riata at the cattle. "Hunt 'em down."

The words were a signal. Amigo crouched, head level and threatening. He looked vicious, as if he'd savage any stragglers that didn't run.

The cattle burst into a rocking, splashing gallop. Like tightrope walkers, they balanced side to side, heading for the safety of the wild side of the river.

As soon as the cattle ran, Dallas spun Amigo on his hind legs, then dismounted. He set the reins over the horse's head.

"Go on home, 'Migo."

The old horse moved off at a shambling trot and Dallas watched every step.

"Now," the foreman said, "tell me about that 'sorry' part while we walk back to the ranch."

After they rubbed down the horses, Dallas went to the bunkhouse to change and told Sam he'd meet her in the ranch house kitchen as soon as he had.

It was only one thirty in the afternoon, but overcast skies and a power failure made the house feel as if night were coming on.

Sam grabbed a flannel shirt, fresh jeans, and turned the shower on full blast. She took off her muddy clothes and stepped into the shower, turned her face to the spray, then lathered her hair.

It might be her last peaceful moment for a long time. Even if Dallas didn't know she was grounded, he had to tell Gram and Dad she'd almost drowned. Or did he?

A flash flood was an act of nature, totally unpredictable, right? She sighed. She knew the answer was no.

Sam was ready to rinse the suds from her hair when the water slowed, dwindled to a stream no bigger than a pencil, then stopped altogether.

Why? She'd never been alone when this had happened. She'd left this sort of problem to Dad. She concentrated.

Their water heater ran on propane, but . . .

"The pump runs on electricity, stupid!" Sam's voice echoed around her.

Only the water left standing in the pipes had run out in the shower, and she'd used it up fast. She was clean enough, but what was she supposed to do with her soapy hair?

"How long have you lived here?" she muttered to her foamy-topped reflection in the mirror.

Blaze's toenails came clicking upstairs. He stood panting outside the bathroom door.

Blaze hadn't let himself into the house, so Dallas must be downstairs waiting. She'd have to hurry if she didn't want to make him even more annoyed.

In three minutes flat, Sam was dressed and downstairs with a towel wrapped turban-style around her hair. Her stomach was growling so loud, she wondered why Blaze didn't answer it.

She brought a plate of cookies to the table. She had just put a cookie in her mouth when Dallas asked, "Was he there?"

Shocked, Sam stopped chewing. Dallas seemed to know exactly where she'd gone, and why.

"That's all I'm going to ask." He stared down at his folded hands. "And if you decide to tell me anything else I might have to call Wyatt. Otherwise, I'm thinking you went out riding this morning, got caught in a flash flood, but had the good judgment to try to take care of seven or eight head of cattle and wait for help."

Sam's tired brain sorted back through the list. Riding. Flash flood. Cattle.

"That's right," Sam said, and it was so. There wasn't a single lie in Dallas's list—if he didn't ask where she'd ridden out *from* this morning. "But I—"

Dallas held a palm toward her and Sam stopped talking. The foreman knew the Phantom's freedom, and maybe his life, were at stake. He cared, but he didn't want her confession.

Sam fidgeted in her chair. Would any harm be caused by keeping where she'd slept a secret?

"No, he wasn't there." Sam circled back to Dallas's question. "I think Karla Starr's got him."

"She might."

"And since that's against the law, and BLM is in charge of watching out for mustangs, I think I should call Brynna Olson and tell her that I saw the Phantom's herd and he wasn't with them."

Dallas nodded.

"And then . . ." Sam wondered just how much of a buddy Dallas was willing to be. "And then, I thought I'd figure out which rodeo Karla Starr is supplying stock for this weekend"—Sam met Dal's blue eyes; he hadn't said no yet—"and have you, uh, drive me there?"

"Right now. During a major storm. Without Wyatt's permission."

"No, we could call Dad first. I have the phone number of the motel."

"And you think he'd say it's fine and dandy?"

"Well, if they weren't too far away." Sam counted three cookie crumbs on the table. "And if I was with you." She used her finger to herd the crumbs together. "Yeah, I think he'd say it was all right."

Dallas shook his head. "You know, I remember when you couldn't hold up your head. Now you're maneuverin' me into running all over the countryside on a wild-goose chase."

The electricity chose that moment to return. If the lights hadn't flashed bright and the television clicked on with a chorus of recorded laughter, things might have been different.

But Sam took the sudden gaiety as a sign. And so, it seemed, did Dallas. Or maybe he was simply too tired to argue.

"Okay." Dallas pushed back from the kitchen table. He took a green coffee can from the cupboard and ran water into a small tin coffeepot. "Get on the phone, sweet talker, and let's see what you can work out."

Chapter Fifteen ❧

Of course, Gram and Dad weren't in their motel room.

Even if they'd heard about the flash flood, it was Saturday. Gram would be frying chicken in her neat white apron. Dad would be riding Banjo in lazy figure eights, warming him up for the roping competition. So Sam left a message.

"Dad, Gram, please tell Brynna that the Phantom isn't with his herd." Sam's voice stayed level. Since Dallas had agreed to help her, she felt strong.

"There's a young black stallion who thinks he's in charge. He must be the Phantom's son, because he looks just like Blackie did." Sam thought for a few seconds.

"That's all, I guess. There was kind of a lot of flooding, but Dallas can tell you about that tonight. 'Bye. I love you."

Sam ran upstairs and rinsed her hair. Then, still

hungry, Sam put a frying pan on the stove, turned on the burner, and made a grilled cheese sandwich.

"Are you sure you don't want one?" she asked as butter sizzled on the hot pan.

"Not good for my old heart." Dallas shook his head and sipped his fresh coffee. "And you seem dead-set on testing it."

While the bread browned and the cheese melted, Sam called the number of the BLM corrals at Willow Springs. No one answered, since it was Saturday afternoon.

Sam wasn't surprised. She'd known since daybreak that Brynna was her only hope. Brynna wanted the stallion left on the range to improve the mustangs of the Calico Mountains. And Brynna had the authority to notify rangers when something was wrong.

Dallas munched an apple while Sam ate, and together they listened to the radio. No flash flood or storm warnings were reported, and even the storm watch had ended. Dry and clear on Sunday, the weatherman said, with temperatures predicted to be around 68 degrees.

Outside the kitchen window, though, it was still windy and gray.

Sam started for the sink to wash her dishes.

"Leave those for now," Dallas said.

"Really?" Sam backed away from the sink.

How cool of Dallas to let her relax. Maybe she'd kindle a blaze in the fireplace and start on that history

project for real. It would be cozy, sipping hot chocolate and reading while the fire baked the rain chill
from her bones.

"You can do dishes later." Dal took his hat from
the hook by the door. "We've got near three hours of
daylight left. Before we go gallavantin' off to rodeos,
we gotta make those cattle as safe as possible. I'll
catch Strawberry and Jeeper. You be out front in five
minutes."

From the River Bend bridge, Sam saw that the
river had receded faster than it had risen.

Sculpted by floodwater, the riverbank dirt wore
ripply patterns. In low places, puddles shone. Sticks,
rocks, and clumps of brush were strewn at the high-
water mark.

The cottonwood tree was missing a few lower
branches, but once more it stood beside the river,
instead of in the middle. Two jays hopped on its
branches, squawking.

Sam surveyed the ranch. If this flood had rushed
through San Francisco, she and Aunt Sue would be
staring out the apartment window, looking down on
cleanup efforts. Red and amber lights would flash,
backup warnings would beep from emergency vehicles, and workers in hard hats would string cables
everywhere.

Here, nature had started healing both animals
and land.

Sam's heart hurt as she remembered the Phantom

wasn't out there, tending his herd.

Hooves splashed, and for one soaring second Sam hoped the stallion had come to prove her wrong. Instead, she saw Pepper and Ross riding toward her and Dallas.

"Been upstream as far as Three Ponies?" Dallas asked.

Ross nodded. "Just—" He pointed at the debris left behind, indicating there was no more serious damage.

Sam pushed her damp bangs out of her eyelashes. If she hadn't been so tired, she would have teased Ross. The shy cowboy never wasted a word when he could use a gesture.

Pepper, all red hair and energy, sat on a fretting Quarter horse named Nike. Pepper wasn't much older than Jake, but he was a full-time cowboy and proud he'd bought the lanky horse he called a "ruby bay" with his own earnings. The animal suited him, Sam thought. Neither of them ever settled down.

Just now, though, Sam felt Pepper checking her out.

"Hey there, cowgirl, you look pretty done in."

It was as close as Pepper would come to questioning Dallas's judgment about making Sam work. Always the boss, Dallas just turned Jeeper downstream and rode on.

"'Course, we don't have Jake." Pepper reined Nike into step with Strawberry. "I guess we can make do with you."

Sam smiled. It was the kind of compliment only a cowboy would give, and she accepted it with pride.

The four riders fanned out across the range on both sides of the river. Their eyes searched everywhere for cows in trouble.

They didn't see many. After days of being herded to higher ground, most cattle had stayed in the upper valleys, even though it contradicted their usual grazing patterns.

Sam surprised five deer drinking from a puddle that a red-winged blackbird was using as a bathtub. The does raised their muzzles, judging Sam with gentle eyes before they pranced away. And then she saw the dead heifer.

Sam didn't want to look. She tried to believe the bloated cow was something else. A rust-colored sofa, maybe, jammed there between a ripped-off branch and a boulder.

Was it her fault? Was this one of the two heifers who'd leaped ahead of her and Ace, then been snatched off their hooves and washed downriver? Why did she have to find this corpse?

It wasn't fair. She wasn't a cowboy, she was a kid. Then Sam reminded herself that this wasn't punishment. It was part of ranching. Here, even a teenager had to pitch in and help.

Sam urged Strawberry forward, overriding the mare's caution.

"Pepper!" Sam yelled to him, since he was nearest.

"Want to give me a hand?"

Coming at a jog, Pepper limbered up his rope. He'd already seen the cow. He didn't offer Sam a word of sympathy, but she heard it in the respect he gave the dead animal.

"I'll just put a loop on this old girl and bring her back where she belongs." Pepper sent his rope flying.

Though it took several tries, a loop finally tightened around two stiff hind legs. Eyes rolling, nostrils fluttering in disgust, Nike pulled the awful burden to shore.

By dusk the cowboys had dragged home three dead Herefords wearing River Bend brands.

Standing in the ranch yard at last, Sam's arms felt too limp to lift the saddle from Strawberry's back. She did it anyway.

"It's a sad business," Dallas admitted. He looked out to the far pasture, where Ross was using their beat-up bulldozer to bury the dead cattle. "But we didn't find that calico-faced heifer you mentioned. Maybe she grew fins."

Sam managed a smile just before she heard the phone.

Thinking of the Phantom, she ran for it.

"'Bout time you got in." Dad sounded mad. "What's all this about a flood and how is it you're not sitting home studying so you can answer the phone?"

"They needed me—Pepper, Dallas, and Ross

did—and I—." Sam shrugged out of her slicker and let it fall on the kitchen floor. "Some of our cows drowned, Dad, and—Ace did his best, you know? We tried to keep them from jumping in, but—"

"You were out there on Ace?" Dad's voice shook.

"—there were pieces of fence and branches and whirlpools." Sam kept talking, trying to make him understand. "They couldn't swim because the water was going so fast, even where it was only a few inches deep. It looked like chocolate milk, all churned up, and it snatched their feet right out from under them."

Dad had stayed quiet too long. Sam picked up the slicker from the floor and hung it, as if he were watching. Had Dad figured out from her message that she'd ridden alone to the Phantom's valley?

The long-distance line crackled with static.

"Did you and Gram win?" she asked weakly.

"Samantha, you're not making one bit of sense. Let me talk with Dal, if he's there."

"Yes sir, he's just outside. I'll get him."

I'm dead. Sam lay the receiver down and shuffled outside.

She felt dizzy. Pepper and Dallas looked like a black-and-white photo of the Old West. Standing in the dusk, they looked at her over the backs of tired horses.

"Dad wants to talk with you."

Both Blaze and Dallas followed Sam inside, and Sam kept walking. She sat on the living room floor in front of the television. She stared at the screen without noticing what she was watching, and petted Blaze's head until he fell asleep.

Something in Dallas's tone changed, attracting her attention.

"Three. She was right," Dallas said. "Yeah, she got a good scare, but . . . Naw, she's fine. Could use some sleep.

"The thing is . . ." Dallas's voice dropped almost to a whisper for what seemed like a long time. " . . . Sweetwater, Riverton, and someplace near Salt Lake. 'Course, that one's out."

As Sam pushed off the floor and tried to stand, her knees stuck. Her leg muscles trembled, too. Without thinking, she must have clamped them hard around Ace to keep from falling into the raging waters. Poor Ace.

She wobbled toward the kitchen and braced in the door frame. Why pretend she wasn't eavesdropping? Dal knew she was, or he wouldn't have whispered.

Water had dripped off Dal's slicker and made a pool around his boots. He must have been concentrating awfully hard not to have noticed.

"Weather station says it's passed on through." Dallas was nodding. "Nothing the boys can't handle. Okay, you have yourself a nice evening, now. Eat some of that fettuccine alfredo for me, and don't worry about a thing. I'll send her off to bed early and see you all sometime tomorrow night."

Dallas hung up.

Sam waited.

Then, all the wrinkles on Dallas's tanned face lifted and he gave Sam a thumbs-up and a smile that made her whoop for joy.

Dad had said they could go.

She crossed all her fingers on both hands. This time tomorrow, the Phantom could be home, safe and sound.

Sam had turned off her reading light. Her eyes were closed and her mind drifting, when the telephone rang. She stared stupidly at the numbers on her watch. Nine o'clock. She peered toward the dark outside her window. Nine o'clock at night. She really had conked out early.

Oh, ow! Sam tottered across her bedroom floor and into the hall, but her leg muscles were so stiff she had to cling to the banister to make it downstairs.

The phone was still ringing when she entered the kitchen, so the call must be important.

"Hello?"

"You sound outta breath." Jake's lazy voice made Sam sure he'd taken all those naps she'd only dreamed of today. "Were you in the barn?"

"No, I was in bed."

"Are you okay? Did you hurt yourself in the flood?"

"Did *I* hurt . . . *myself*?" Sam's fingers clamped hard on the telephone receiver. "Let me think."

She thought of shale sliding on slick mud, of cattle rocketing against Ace so he nearly stumbled into the wild river, of wind and rain that might have added up to hypothermia.

"No, I didn't hurt myself. Thanks for asking."

"Whew, you've sure got your cranky pants on tonight."

"My, my—*what*?"

Jake laughed at Sam's outrage. Then he used an adult voice meant to put her in her place. "I only called to see how Teddy's doing."

Sam winced. She should have thought of the Curly Bashkir colt Jake was schooling sooner. The two-year-old was at a critical stage in his training, and no one had ridden him since Jake's accident.

"He's fine. We put him in the ten-acre pasture and he's getting along with the other horses. In fact, he and Jeepers are sort of palling around together."

"That's good. I was thinking . . ." Jake's voice trailed off. He cleared his throat.

"My alarm is set for four A.M.," she said, "so if this is going to take long—"

"Zip it, Sam. You know I'm bad at asking for favors. What I was thinking, though, is that Monday, if I can get Nate or somebody to drive me over, you could work Teddy while I tell you what to do."

"Like *that* would be a new experience."

"Forget I asked."

"No, I won't." Sam wondered if she could use this as an excuse to put off Rachel's lesson. "Of course I'll do it. I'm flattered you asked."

"Who else is there?"

Sam laughed in spite of herself. "You're a great guy, Ely, but I'm going back to bed. Good night."

The receiver was almost down when she heard him ask, "Where are you going at four A.M.?"

For some reason of its own, Sam's brain flashed a picture of Rachel's arms linked around Jake's waist as they rode double.

"To my friend Duncan's house," Sam said.

"Duncan? Duncan *who*?"

Sam hung up the phone. She didn't go back and answer its ring as she walked upstairs, either.

Of course, she didn't have a friend named Duncan, but that didn't matter. It served Jake right.

Ahh. Sam's shaky muscles unfurled as she got back into bed. When her head touched the pillow, she was in heaven.

Even though her alarm was set for four A.M., Sam's lips curved in the biggest grin she'd worn all day.

Chapter Sixteen ॐ

Sam came downstairs before dawn and found Dallas hunched over road maps of California, Nevada, and Utah.

"Last night I called the stock manager at Karla Starr's ranch. I told him we had animals she might be interested in—which is true."

Sam nodded. If Dark Sunshine hadn't been in foal, she knew Karla Starr would have made an offer. She also knew that had nothing to do with Dallas's call.

"Her manager says Karla moves around a lot— one step ahead of the law, I'm guessing."

Dallas's guess brought Sam fully awake. If Karla Starr had the Phantom, he'd be stolen property.

"In any case, the manager doesn't keep close tabs on her. Just feeds broncs and bulls, but he had a few hunches where she might be this weekend."

Dallas positioned a map so Sam could see.

"We'll be checking the Sweetwater Rodeo first," he said, "since it's closest."

The next closest was a hundred miles beyond Sweetwater, at the Wild West Days rodeo in Riverton, California.

"Third place is a college rodeo in Tower Mountain, Utah, but that's too far to check and still be back in time for school Monday morning."

Dallas folded the Utah map, put it away, and ten minutes later they were on the road.

Sam had never seen a more beautiful sunrise than the one over the rodeo grounds in Sweetwater, Nevada. The glitter of sun on windshields in the contestants' parking lot made yesterday's storm seem like nothing but a bad dream.

Although the rodeo wouldn't start until noon, cowboys and cowgirls were crawling out of campers and motor homes, checking on their horses, and looking for breakfast.

Some followed their noses toward the pancake breakfast served after a church service held in the arena.

"Kinda peaceful, isn't it?" Dallas stretched as he climbed out of the truck.

Sam nodded. She'd never been to rodeo grounds before the action began. An event program somersaulted in the wind, and the grandstands overlooking the arena were empty.

"You'd never guess at all the music, yelling, bucking, and bellowin' that'll be startin' up soon," Dallas mused. "But this is a good time for us to look around, see if we can find Karla Starr's fancy truck or anything else with her brand on it."

Dallas strode past a maze of metal fences and gates, and Sam followed.

"All those go somewhere," Dallas said. "The trick is to get the bulls and broncs headed for the right chute and the cowboy who drew 'em."

Dallas explained that a cowboy registered for an event and then his name was randomly matched with a certain animal.

"At small shows like this, their names are probably just drawn from a hat. In big rodeos, they use a computer."

"Pretty high-tech," Sam said. "But does it really matter which one you get?"

"Sure does," Dallas said. "If you get one that bucks and you stay on, you make lots of points and money. A stock contractor's dream is an animal that bucks hard every time. All the cowboys want to draw him."

Sam closed her eyes in dismay. The Phantom would buck until his proud heart broke.

"Over here." Dallas steered Sam around a bare-chested cowboy whose ribs were being wrapped with yards of white tape. "Those are the holding pens."

A dozen horses raised their heads from a pile of

hay. Still chewing, they regarded Sam and Dallas.

"Those don't look like wild horses."

"They're not on the job," Dallas explained, then added, "and not one of 'em looks like your Phantom."

He was right. Except for one black and one paint, all the horses in this pen were bays and sorrels.

"So, do we give up and go on to the next one?" Sam asked.

"Not just yet." Dallas's hands perched on his hips. He scanned the closed concession booths painted with pictures of cotton candy and corn dogs.

Professional stock contractors, Dallas explained, had many responsibilities and lots of rules to follow at sanctioned rodeos.

But this wasn't a sanctioned rodeo, and Karla Starr fell short of being a professional.

"Sanctioned means approved, right?" Sam asked. "Who sanctions them?"

"At small, end-of-the-season rodeos like this one, it's hard to tell. All those the manager mentioned were connected with county fairs and such." Dallas shook his head as if he'd expected as much. "The bigger rodeos, though, for cowboys who're tryin' to make a living, are sanctioned by professional cowboy organizations. That's how they get points and honors and whatnot."

The aromas of sausage and pancakes made Sam hungry, but keeping up with Dallas kept her from thinking about it too much.

Cowboys and cowgirls were lined up at a folding table shaded by a picnic umbrella. They were paying entry fees and getting starting times for the day's events, Dal explained.

Every time they saw the bobbing ears or shiny hindquarters of a horse, they detoured to take a look. The rodeo grounds were growing busy. Trucks and cars pulled in. Trailer gates were opened and restless horses unloaded. Dogs and children scattered, looking for companions.

Once, Sam sprinted toward a rearing gray horse, only to find she was really an Appaloosa.

"She hates having her legs taped," a girl explained to Sam. "But it keeps her from getting banged up."

Next, they passed a bull fighter. He wore clownish clothes and makeup, but his leg was extended and a woman dressed like a paramedic was wrapping it with tape matched to his athletic shoes.

"Everywhere I look, somebody's getting bandaged up," Sam said. "It looks like a hospital back here."

"Rodeo's a rough game," Dallas agreed.

Before they gave up, Dallas even checked the chutes that opened into the arena. They were empty, but Sam couldn't help noticing that inside them, the wooden walls were gouged through the paint, down to bare wood.

"Some poor horse—"

"Or some poor cowboy," Dallas corrected.

"Yeah, but the cowboys have a choice."

"Ya got me there," Dallas agreed, but he seemed

to be thinking of something else.

Sam crossed her arms and considered a pen of bucking bulls. They looked healthy and well fed. One dozed in the sun.

She wished she could sleep through these mixed feelings. She'd always loved the popcorn smell and excitement of rodeos, but the thought of the Phantom, terrified and confused, changed everything.

"I have one more idea." Dallas strode toward a man with a clipboard and a walkie-talkie. "Excuse me, can you give me an idea of when the wild horse race starts?"

The man didn't bother consulting his papers. "We don't have one here at Sweetwater, but you could probably catch the one in Riverton. I hear they've put all their local businessmen in teams of three to compete against each other." He chuckled and swept a hand over the small, busy fairgrounds. "That'd give us about one team."

Sam tried to talk with Dal as he hurried toward the truck. "What's a wild horse race?"

Now the smell of onion rings mingled with the smell of pancakes and sausage, making her even hungrier, but Sam still caught Dallas's answer.

"You'll see when we get there," he snapped, and something in his tone told Sam she wouldn't like what she saw.

Halfway to Riverton, Dallas stopped for gasoline. Inside the convenience store, he bought them microwaved burritos and colas.

"For heaven's sake, don't tell your Gram."

"I won't," Sam promised. Gram thought fast food was corrupting the younger generation.

"You want one of those fried pies, too?" Dallas pointed at little greasy things that didn't look anything like Gram's pies.

"Can I have ice cream instead?" Sam felt greedy after she said it.

"I don't mind spoilin' you some." Dallas laughed. "You were a big help yesterday. Get anything you want, just so long as you can eat it in the truck."

Riverton's Wild West Days rodeo was in full swing when they arrived. They hurried to the arena just as saddle bronc riding was announced.

A pale horse spun in the middle of a dust cloud. With the sun shining through, Sam couldn't tell the color of his coat.

When the buzzer sounded, the cowboy's free arm stopped waving and a pickup man swooped in on a sturdy Quarter horse. Smoothly, he yanked at the bronc's flank cinch and helped the rider to the ground.

The bronc stopped bucking and ran for an open gate. His coat was a creamy palomino.

"I thought for a minute . . ."

"Too polished," Dallas said. "That palomino's been in a chute more than a time or two."

The announcer boomed the name of the next cowboy and a horse called TNT, but there was a commotion in the chute and they didn't emerge.

Maybe, Sam thought, *maybe this is him.*

It wasn't. The horse exploding out of the chute was dark, the color of a bruise. He seemed to fly.

"A sun fisher," Dallas said. "See how he twists up in the air so the sun shines on his belly? And that"— he pointed as the cowboy flew off over the horse's tail—"is called goin' out the back door."

Sam admired the skilled horsemanship of the pickup men. She appreciated Dallas's explanations and his offer of cotton candy, but she was losing hope.

Dallas must have noticed.

"I'm thinking the Phantom—if he's here at all— will be in the wild horse race. He'd be a devil to get in one of those chutes, and besides"—Dallas looked around the fairgrounds as if instinct was whispering to him—"they might not be too careful checking brands on horses that're supposed to act wild."

Sam and Dallas left the stands to search the holding pens.

They wandered through the dust, checking everywhere.

Unlike the Sweetwater rodeo, action was all around them here. Ropers practiced on anything that moved. A barrel racer's horse, eager to dash into the arena, nearly trampled them. As they sidled into an area behind the chutes, a cowboy grunted. Sam snuck a look just as he leaned down to check a bull rider's spur that had been molded on as part of a smudged and autographed cast.

"Can you believe that?" Sam gasped. The cowboy clearly had a broken leg, and yet he planned to ride.

"Sure." Dallas nodded. "Jake'd ride, if he could get away with it."

Sam guessed Dallas was right, but as they walked among the men preparing for the bull-riding competition, she decided they were insane. She could imagine riding a bucking horse. In fact, she'd done it, just not on purpose.

But bulls scared her. The best were "rank," Dal said. They spun, fought, twisted, and kicked, then chased down the riders with murderous rage.

Sam was listening to a cowboy with a black eye brag that he'd earned it when a bull's horn hooked him, when Dal's voice interrupted.

"You feel like a break?"

For the first time all day, Sam really looked at the foreman. There was a gray cast to his skin, and he shifted from boot to boot, as if neither foot was up to bearing weight.

She'd been selfish, but if she fussed over Dallas he'd keep going, even if he was ready to drop.

"Yeah, I could really go for some lemonade, and maybe we could sit in the shade for a few minutes."

Dal's raised brow made Sam worry that she'd

overdone the pitiful act, but he jerked a thumb toward one of the booths.

It was three o'clock, and Sam had started worrying about Ace—the gelding was bound to be as sore as she was—when a voice announced the wild horse race.

"How they do it," Dal explained carefully, "is put men in teams of three behind a rope barrier. All the wild horses, they put in a chute. There's a whistle, usually, and then the men and horses kinda meet up in the arena."

Sam and Dal found seats in the stands, and before Dallas finished, the announcer's booming voice explained that each team must stop a wild horse and saddle him. Then one man must ride the horse over a finish line.

Three against one, Sam thought as eight horses charged into the arena. None were grays and none looked like mustangs. Probably, they were saddle and bareback broncs, just called "wild" for this event.

No fair. Sam noticed each horse wore a halter with a trailing rope. It made them easier to catch, but when the men grabbed the ropes, holding them out, Sam was afraid one of the spooked horses would come barreling through, trying to escape a pursuer, and trip.

A perfect event for the Phantom. No experience required, just energy and speed.

One team had its horse. The paint struggled as a

man hung on his head and another chased him with the saddle.

Sam didn't realize she was holding her face in her hands until the third man dodged the paint's heels and twisted its tail. Pain made the horse still, and the saddle crashed down upon his back. Before any of the men could mount, Sam covered her eyes.

"I don't think he's here," Dallas said, standing up. "'Bout time for us to be going anyway."

Dallas led the way back to the truck. They were already on the freeway, headed home, when Sam spoke.

"I don't know what to hope—that Karla has him, but just didn't bring him to this rodeo, or that the black stallion killed him, or that he just deserted his herd . . ."

"Not likely." Dallas stared at the road ahead.

Sam knew she should let him concentrate. He didn't drive in heavy traffic very often.

"If I turn on the radio," Dal said, "think you could still grab some sleep?"

"Sure," she said, but it didn't happen. When Dallas spoke again, Sam was still awake.

"You and me don't have the manpower to go after Karla Starr the way she deserves," Dallas said, as if he'd been thinking about the Phantom for the whole hour they'd been driving. "Much as I hate to say it, BLM might be the stallion's best hope."

"Maybe." Sam looked out the window. As they

traveled on, she saw mud on the pavement, and water ran in channels next to the road.

There would still be flood damage to deal with at home. So she'd have lots to think about besides the Phantom.

What's next?

Sam didn't know she'd whispered the words until Dallas answered.

"What's next is this: Get that Brynna Olson on your side. Wyatt says she's half as crazy for that stallion as you are, and that's crazy enough to defend him like a mother bear."

Chapter Seventeen ⟩

$\mathcal{G}$ram and Dad still weren't home from the fair when Sam and Dallas pulled into the ranch yard long after dark, but Pepper met them with good news.

"All night long the local TV news has been sayin' Darton High School is closed Monday." Pepper was hatless and his red hair stuck out in clumps, but he looked happy for her.

"Why is it closed?" Sam rejoiced at the chance to do her homework tomorrow, instead of doing it half-asleep tonight. Then an awful thought cropped up. "The library's not flooded, is it?"

Though most of Darton High was ordinary, Sam loved the library. Tall windows kept it sunny, and a librarian with a green thumb coaxed ferns and flowers to brighten every corner.

"They didn't mention it." Pepper rubbed his eyes, then yawned. "Just said the road was washed out, like it is lots of places in town."

"Thanks for staying up to tell me. Now I can go out and check on Ace."

"He's fine. They're all fine, and 'cept for those three heifers, the cattle seem to have made it through."

Sam's arms felt heavy and the barn looked far away.

"Sam, honest." Pepper must have seen her weariness. "I looked Ace over."

"I know," Sam said as she started walking, "but he needs to know I'm home."

Ace neighed a sweet welcome, and Sam ran the rest of the way. "You look pretty good, but you wouldn't turn down a massage, would you?" Sam took up the rubber curry comb and worked it over Ace's coat. He shook his mane as if her touch gave him chills of delight.

"I didn't find the Phantom," Sam confessed. "Ace, what if I never do?"

She kept brushing long after his bay coat shone. Then she told Ace the truth that had ached inside her for three long days.

"It's my fault. I let him become too tame." Sam remembered how close the stallion had come that day when Rachel had been lost. "Dad was right, but I didn't believe him until it was too late. The Phantom would be curious about Karla and get too close. Then I bet she caught him herself."

Sam dropped the curry comb and leaned against

Ace's back. "I'm to blame," she whispered, "and I don't know what to do."

Ace didn't have any answers, but talking to him helped more than crying. Finally, Sam went to the house and left the front porch light on. She was ready for sleep.

Gram woke her with a kiss and a glass of orange juice.

Sam struggled up on her elbows. Gram snatched a tee-shirt from Sam's floor and straightened some papers that didn't need straightening. Sam had missed her.

"You won, huh?"

Gram turned, a towel dangling from her fingers, and smiled. "I did, and not only a blue ribbon but two hundred dollars' credit at the new superstore in Darton."

"That's great. What are you going to buy? A rice cooker?"

Gram had been reading up on those appliances for months. She loved making Asian food, but she just didn't have the knack with rice that she had with potatoes and breads.

"Land sakes, no. I'll just put it toward our monthly food bill and it'll be gone quick enough." Gram's words drifted back as she bustled out the door.

Sam slipped out of bed and dressed, thinking

about Gram. The trip and the blue ribbon were reward enough for her, it seemed, but shouldn't she buy herself a treat, too?

"Wyatt's in the barn," Gram said as Sam poured her cereal. "He wants to talk with you."

"About what?"

"You'll have to ask him." Gram frowned at Sam's breakfast. "You should have some fruit on that, at least. And some whole-wheat toast." Gram held out a hand to ward off Sam's protest. "Even if you're not hungry."

Dad was in the barn talking with Dallas, but Tank stood saddled at the rail, so Dad had probably already ridden out to look over the storm-damaged range.

Sam heard Dad's voice before she saw him.

"It wasn't a decision I made quick, but what he offered for Banjo, after we won, was just about the price those three heifers would've brought at market. And that's if it had been a good market."

"You sold Banjo?" Sam stepped into the barn. She couldn't believe Dad had meant what he'd said.

He didn't answer right away, and maybe it was a good thing. The look he gave her was complicated and it took her a minute to figure out. His expression said he was glad she was alive, that he would've liked a greeting instead of an accusation, and that her eavesdropping was out of line for a thirteen-year-old.

But all Dad said was, "Yes, I did."

"But, Dad, you love that horse."

"No. I love this ranch and the people on it." Dad's eyes wouldn't let her wiggle away. "Banjo's a good horse, but I have others. He made lots of contributions to this ranch."

"I heard he won," Sam admitted, "and you got enough to balance things."

"More than that. After I sold him, I felt sorta at loose ends. Your Gram was in a runoff for first place." Dad's grin flashed, then faded. "I went to a workshop the county was givin' and learned about drought-tolerant hay and grass seed that grows in poor soil."

"I'm sorry, Dad." Sam saw Dallas slip out of the barn to give them privacy. "I didn't mean to sound—" She shrugged. No word really fit.

"It's hard. I know." Dad placed a hand on Sam's shoulder. "And I'm sorry as I can be that your Phantom's gone."

"You know what, though?" Sam felt suddenly excited. Now that Brynna was back, things might change for the better. "Dallas said I should get Brynna busy on this. Do you think it's too early to call?"

"She'll be in her office by now." Dad smiled, looking a little awkward. "Sam, about Brynna. We need to talk."

"I know. Me and my big mouth. Dad, I'm really sorry I was rude to her the other day, but I do trust her. I think she's the only one who can help."

Dad took off his Stetson, smoothed his hair, then put his hat on again. "Go ahead and call her."

Brynna was at Willow Springs, but she took ten whole minutes to come to the phone.

"Sam." Brynna sounded exasperated when she finally picked up. "If it were anybody but you, I'd tell you to go fly a kite. I'm awfully busy with the Red Rock horses we had to bring in because of drought, and now there's another twenty or so on their way — in bad shape from the flood."

"Gee, I'm sorry. If I can—"

"So, what I'm saying, Sam"—Brynna's tone was half impatience and half amusement—"is 'spit it out, honey, or I'm going to hang up this dang phone.'"

It wasn't the encouragement Sam had hoped for, but she tried. "You got my message about the Phantom, right?"

"I did. I feel awful." Brynna paused before her brisk professional manner kicked in, full force. "But I must rule out natural causes—predators, injuries, and the like—before questioning Karla Starr."

"I already did that—ruled out other causes."

"No offense, Sam, but no, you have not. And it's going to be a solid week before I can release rangers for that purpose. I'm sor—Just a minute."

Brynna muffled the mouthpiece, then returned. "Sam, I've got to go. If it's possible, I'll be out at River

Bend tonight and we'll talk more." She paused as commotion continued in her office. "I may be late."

Dallas needed Sam's help riding upstream. A big piece of bank had caved in, narrowing the river's flow, and Sam spent most of the afternoon with a shovel.

Only when she saw the baby blue Mercedes bumping across the bridge did she realize Rachel had come for her lesson even though school had been canceled.

Sam didn't allow herself to complain, even mentally. Gram was using her prize money for groceries and Dad had sold Banjo to cover the cost of the lost cattle. The least she could do was watch Rachel trot around in circles on Ace.

Dallas saw the car and waved Sam toward home. "C'mon, Strawberry." Sam urged the mare into a lope toward the house. "I'll work on my blisters later on."

Sam figured she must have been too busy shoveling mud to see the Elys drop Jake off, but there he was, laughing and talking with Rachel.

Sam drew rein and watched.

Hopping around on his good leg, Jake had managed to saddle Teddy, and it looked as if Rachel had been mirroring his efforts with Ace. She sure didn't laugh like that when Sam told her which strap went through which ring. And she'd never saddled up so fast.

Okay, so Jake had been cooped up for a week. Even Rachel probably seemed like good company after that.

Ace neighed a welcome, although Sam felt invisible to Jake.

"Glad you made it back." Jake frowned as if they'd had an agreement to meet at a certain time.

As if he had so many important engagements to keep.

But Sam didn't say anything out loud. She wasn't sure why, but it had something to do with Rachel.

"Let me slip Stawberry's bit out and let out her cinch." Sam swung down and loosened things, so the mare would be more comfortable while she waited. Dallas had said they might have to go out again later.

It was bad enough that Rachel wore perfect jeans and a pink blouse with little pearl studs, while Sam had mud caked on her shirt cuffs and probably in her hair.

"Jake tells me *he* is going to act as master of the horse today." Rachel batted her eyelashes at Jake.

She really did.

Sam wished Jen had been there to see it. And she couldn't wait to tell her how Jake had put Rachel in her place. Except . . . Jake didn't.

Things got worse as the lesson progressed.

"Good job taking him through the barrels at a walk, Rachel. Now try lifting his head a little. No, it's not your fault. He's just being lazy."

Lazy? Ace? But when Sam would have said something, Jake waved a hand her way.

"Keep Teddy back a little."

No *please*. No *thank you*. Just do it, and Jake made no mention of her superb handling of Teddy, a half-trained colt.

"Jog now," Jake ordered.

Where did he think he was, in a show ring?

"Rachel, you'll need to sit down right in the saddle. That's it." Jake leaned against his crutch, smiling.

"No posting in Western, Rachel. I know it's a little uncomfortable at first, but your seat needs to be right in the saddle."

"Rachel's already ridden Ace at a trot," Sam pointed out.

"That's right, I have." Rachel repositioned herself with a thump. Ace braked to a stop and Rachel fell off.

Sam wasn't sure how it happened, but Ace didn't walk off, and Rachel didn't stand up, so Sam dismounted and went to her.

"Why did you do that?" Sam asked.

"Oh, shut up." Rachel's British accent had never sounded so lofty. She took a quick glance at Jake, then lowered her voice. "You think you're so smart about horses. Well, why didn't you brand that stallion if he was yours?"

Sam stood speechless for a minute. Rachel had to be talking about the Phantom, but why?

"I wanted him wild," Sam snapped, even before

she could question Rachel's sudden change in topic.

"Well, if you wanted him at all, you should have bloody well done it."

"Ladies?" Jake called. "How 'bout another ride along the rail, then reverse and . . ."

If the baby blue Mercedes had been bringing serum for a fatal disease, Sam couldn't have been happier to see it. She only wished Mrs. Coley would take Jake away, too.

Alone, Sam unsaddled all three horses and brushed them. Before putting Ace away, she checked his feet and found a pebble in his off hind hoof. Of course Rachel wouldn't have noticed.

Sam had put Ace in his corral and was leading Teddy and Strawberry out to the ten-acre pasture when Jake finally fell in beside her. She slowed down a little so he could keep up.

She turned both horses out and watched them run. With manes and tails lifting on the late-afternoon wind, they were so beautiful, Sam wanted to cry. Instead, she turned on Jake.

"You don't even like Rachel!" she snapped.

Jake gave a self-satisfied smile.

"You're only nice to her because she's cute!"

His smile got a little broader.

"And I'll tell you, Jake Ely, one more clever remark about her *seat* and I would have lost my lunch!"

Jake was trying not to laugh, but he failed. Sam

socked him in the arm.

"Ow," he said, and laughed harder.

She stared at him, hoping he'd be embarrassed once he got over being so terribly amused.

"You're right. I don't like her." Jake rubbed his arm. "I'm only nice to her because she's paying *you* money, and for crying out loud, do you just ignore her posting?"

If she hadn't heard Mrs. Ely's car coming across the bridge, Sam might have hit him again. For making sense.

Jealousy and Rachel's slashing remarks about the Phantom came together into something dark and mean inside Sam.

"I'm not speaking to you anymore, Jake Ely. Find someone else to make fun of, okay?"

She turned and walked toward the house.

"Oh, Brat, come back here."

Sam lengthened her stride. She held her head up as if a string ran straight up to the stars pricking through the dusky sky.

It felt good to pay him back.

Chapter Eighteen ❧

*B*rynna came for dinner and stayed too long. Sam was in no mood to watch her and Dad give each other slow, meaningful smiles. Gram must have noticed Sam's irritation, because she asked if Sam wouldn't like to take her dessert upstairs and finish her homework.

Just perfect, Sam thought. Her algebra homework was as baffling as this entire day. She was concentrating so hard, she didn't even hear the phone ring.

Dad came upstairs to tell her, "That was Jake on the phone."

Sam almost snapped that she wasn't speaking to Jake Ely. Ever again. But Dad's formal tone stopped her.

"It was?"

"Yeah." Dad stared at a glass horse on one of her shelves. She'd bought him when she was ten, because he looked like Blackie. "Honey, he has a videotape he thinks we all should see."

✳ ✳ ✳

Sam had never left for a neighbor's house this late. Driving through the darkness on a school night might have been fun, except that Brynna was explaining while Dad drove.

"The Elys get the sports channel on their big satellite dish, Sam. Apparently they taped a weekend rodeo wrap-up that included all kinds of highlights, even from dinky little rodeos."

Brynna waited for Sam's brain to brace for what was coming. Finally, she understood.

"Oh no." Sam wanted to cover her ears. "No." She wanted to tell Brynna to stop.

"I'm reserving judgment until I see the tape, but Jake has a good eye for horses, and he thinks, well, that there's something that needs investigation."

"Enough," Dad said. "We're here."

Once, Sam had been to a gathering after a funeral. Sober-faced ranch families had gathered in a living room. They'd balanced plates of food on their knees, but otherwise it had felt just like this.

All the Ely boys sat straight-backed on chairs and couches. They nodded at Sam. A big wooden bowl filled with popcorn sat, forgotten, as they faced the blank TV set.

Mrs. Ely gave Sam a one-armed hug. Jake's dad, Luke, watched her as if he was afraid she might stumble and break into a million pieces. Of course she didn't stumble, or break anything. Unless her heart counted.

First the tape showed clips of a bucking bull spinning until it staggered with dizziness. It showed a calf roper sail over his horse's head and outdistance the running calf.

Those were supposed to be funny, but Sam was so busy lacing her fingers together, to keep them from shaking, that she barely heard the TV announcer's lead-in to the next clip. He said something, she thought, about a young man who'd been injured in a college rodeo.

"This is it," Jake said. "The wild horse race."

Sam wouldn't need a videotape to remember the Phantom's eyes. The photographer had shot from an odd angle, but the stallion's brown mustang eyes, frightened and accusing, stabbed right through her.

And then the camera pulled back. The Phantom was rearing, reaching for the sky, and the rider was falling. *A rider.* Someone—that boy, that stupid, stupid boy—had been on the Phantom's back. Once the boy fell, the Phantom came back to earth.

It made sense. He'd dislodged the attacker.

Except that the boy wouldn't give in. He made a grab for the Phantom's tail, and caught it.

Sam heard a gasp, but she didn't look away from the screen. The Phantom whirled. Mouth agape, he grabbed the boy by the shoulder like he would a misbehaving colt, and shook him.

They'll kill my horse, Sam thought. After that,

they must have shot him.

Sam felt Dad standing beside her as the screen was filled with the face of Karla Starr. Suddenly, Sam knew that the Phantom was more valuable than ever before.

"Starr Productions regrets the injury to Ben Miller." Karla Starr wore thick eye makeup and red lipstick. Fair flags flapped behind her, but her hair didn't move, and Sam remembered what Jen's mom had said about rodeo queens and hair spray. "We deny any accusations that the Renegade is a man-eater. Such things don't exist in the horse world."

Karla Starr moved closer to the microphone and turned steely-eyed. "Rodeo fans can rest assured that when Renegade appears in next Friday's wild horse race, we will prevent such an accident from occurring again."

"Where? *Where?*" Brynna shouted at the television. "Sorry," she said, then threw her French braid over her shoulder and rubbed her palms together before looking at Jake.

"We've played it over and over, Ms. Olson. They don't say."

Sam let Brynna talk to Jake and Nate. She let her consult with Jake's father, who'd spread their coffee table with schedules and charts. He'd already been on the Internet and had Karla Starr's next move narrowed down to five West Coast rodeos.

Sam couldn't stop seeing the Phantom's outrage. The boy had climbed on his back, then grabbed his tail. The stallion was a king in his world. He should never be treated like this.

"Wait." Gram spoke for the first time. "Why don't you just go to her ranch?"

"We will. Tomorrow, first thing." But Brynna was shaking her head even as she said it. "If she has any sense at all, and I'm afraid she does, she won't be there. Or the horse won't.

"We're talking about a federal crime. I don't think she'd hand herself and the stallion to us on a silver platter."

Sam woke the next morning, feeling like her head carried an invisible metal helmet. She wanted to stay home from school, but Dad and Gram said no. It was already Tuesday, they reasoned. In just four days, Karla Starr could be trapped—if she was greedier than she was careful.

It would be better, Gram said, if Sam thought about something else. Like school.

But how could she?

Before facing a breakfast she didn't want, Sam fed the hens. How quickly they'd gotten over the loss of the cottonwood tree. Last week, half their world had turned upside down, and they didn't even remember.

Sam wasn't so lucky. She made it through her morning classes. At lunch, she told a shocked Jen what had happened. But when Mr. Blair gave the journalism class a current events quiz, Sam knew she'd flunked. He'd included no questions about drowned cattle, suffering horses, or people who'd do anything for money.

At home, Sam had a message to call Brynna.

"She's not stupid." Sam could hear Brynna tapping a pencil on her desk at Willow Springs. "Her ranch is in good order and she's got bills of sale on every animal there."

"So, she has him someplace else," Sam said dully. She hoped the Phantom couldn't wonder why this was happening to him.

"Apparently," Brynna said. "We didn't tell her we'd come looking for him. In fact, my ranger just went along with a Humane Society official, as if it were a routine inspection. That way, she may let her guard down and not hide him at the rodeo."

"Do you know which one yet?"

"We're still working on that."

"I want to go with you," Sam insisted.

"Sam, I'll be working."

"If you find him, he'll— Nobody will be able to handle him except me." Sam heard the begging in her own voice, but only part of it was aimed at getting to go. The rest was hope that the Phantom would still love her enough to let her near him.

"I'll talk to your dad," Brynna said finally, and Sam knew that was the best she could hope for.

The Cimmaron County Fair had a great carnival. From miles away, Sam and Brynna saw the neon lights marking the spokes on a Ferris wheel and the swoops of a roller coaster.

As they left the BLM truck in the parking lot, they could already smell hot dogs and funnel cakes and hear the happy shrieks of children on thrill rides.

Brynna carried a small radio she called a "handheld," and she wore a pale blue shirt with jeans. Even out of uniform, she looked official as she surveyed the fairgrounds.

"If we get separated," she told Sam, "this is the midway, there's the exhibit hall, and over there, on the other side of it, are the grandstand and arena. Rodeo security has an office over there."

"I'm not a little kid. I won't wander off." Sam tried not to sound impatient, but Brynna was taking this standing-in-for-Dad responsibility way too seriously. Then again, maybe they were both nervous.

BLM still hadn't found the Phantom. Karla Starr had been contracted to supply stock for the small Cimmaron rodeo, but neither she nor the horse she'd called Renegade had been spotted, so rangers had spread out through three states to watch for the stolen silver stallion.

Brynna was working with local law enforcement, and she really didn't want Sam around during her meetings.

"How 'bout if I buy you dinner?" Brynna looked at the watch she'd actually insisted Sam synchronize to hers. "I've got ten minutes before my meeting, twenty until the grand entry, and another hour or so until the wild horse race. We've got plenty of time."

Sam was scanning the throngs of kids clutching strands of ride tickets. She spotted a familiar face.

Darrell wore a yellow jersey, a backward hat, baggy pants that showed his boxer shorts, and a kid attached to one hand. His irritated expression lifted a little when he saw her.

"Hey, Sam, is Jake with you?"

"No, I'm here with—" Sam caught Brynna's frown. Probably she didn't want Sam to be too specific, but Sam knew she was an awful liar. "With my, uh, aunt."

"What a coincidence, I'm here with my cousin." Darrell held up the hand locked to a freckled boy with untied shoes.

"I wanna go on the Mad Mouse," the child informed Sam.

"That's nice." Sam took a step back. She had on her favorite red blouse, and Darrell's cousin was sticky with what probably had been cotton candy.

"And how old are you?" Brynna asked, but her eyes were sweeping Darrell with disapproval.

"Wanna ride the Mad Mouse," the cousin said again.

"I don't even know what it is," Darrell said. "I'm just here for the drag races after the stupid rodeo ends. This is all Jake's fault, you know. If he was with me, they wouldn't have made me baby-sit."

The child looked up at Darrell. "I wan-na"—he pronounced the words slowly—"go on—"

"I know, I know," Darrell said. "We'll find it. See ya, Sam."

"About dinner," Brynna said. "I don't feel much like it, either, but how about a soda?"

Sam agreed. She watched people throw baseballs at wooden milk bottles and line up for a haunted house that had walls painted with purple-skinned witches.

Finally, Brynna returned with two cherry Cokes and a cardboard envelope of fried artichoke hearts.

"No thanks," Sam said, but Brynna looked so disappointed, she tried one. They weren't bad.

Brynna kept looking at her watch. Sam tried to count people turning green on the Tilt-a-Whirl instead of wondering where Karla Starr had stashed a stallion who should be running wild.

"I've got to go meet Sheriff Rayburn." Brynna tapped her watch face. "Why don't you go wander around the exhibit hall?"

Sam couldn't imagine anything more boring than looking at peaches canned and squares crocheted by 4-H kids she didn't know.

"I think I'll try that for a little while." Sam pointed at a booth where you could throw Ping Pong balls at bowls and win the goldfish inside.

Sam saw Brynna hesitate. "I have money," Sam assured her.

"That's not it." Brynna looked around as if she expected a pack of Darrell look-alikes to swagger up.

"I'm thirteen. As long as we have a place and a time to meet, Dad would let me stay." Sam wasn't sure that was true, but it might be.

"In twenty minutes, I'll meet you right there at the gate." Brynna pointed. "There, where they let the barrel racers in and out, where the grand entry—"

"I see it, and I'll be there in twenty minutes. I promise."

"Karla Starr will probably ride in the grand entry, and I need you to help me spot her," Brynna explained.

"I will. I want to catch her more than anyone does. See you later."

"Samantha, I don't feel good about this." Brynna walked away, still talking. "I'll send rodeo security after you if you're not there."

Heads were turning, so Sam just waved. Brynna had gone past responsible and reached obsessed.

Sam had just decided she'd better quit throwing balls, in case she really did win a goldfish and had to take it home balanced between her ankles on the floor of the truck, when someone tugged on her shirt.

It was Darrell's cousin, and he was crying.

"Are you lost?"

Oh no, don't let him be lost. Sam looked at her watch. Eight minutes until she was supposed to meet Brynna. The cousin kept crying and held his arms out for her to pick him up. What was his name, anyway?

Over the merry-go-round music, she shouted, "Where's Darrell?"

"Mad Mouse," the child moaned, and flung his arms toward her more demandingly.

"Did he leave you at the Mad Mouse or what?" Sam picked up the little boy. When he cuddled his head into her shoulder, she couldn't be too mad at him. But she was going to strangle Darrell.

She balanced the child on her hip and jogged toward the arena. She'd passed the exhibit hall when she heard the rodeo announcer.

"And now for our grand entry."

"Let's go see some horses," Sam said, but running this way was hard, and she wasn't the only one hurrying toward the arena.

Maybe Brynna could send security after Darrell. Except that she didn't see Brynna. The chutes were packed with horses for the first event, saddle bronc riding, and though there were plenty of cowboys stretching their legs, rubbing rosin into their gloves and even praying, she didn't see Brynna.

Sam moved toward the grandstand steps and climbed a few for a better view. No Brynna, but out in the arena the equestrians lined up with flags for the national anthem. There, mounted on a big Quarter horse, sat a rider in aqua sequins with a shooting star on her back.

Karla Starr.

Sam ran back down the stairs.

"Don't bounce!" the child ordered, but she had to find Brynna now.

The arena gates were wide open for the riders to leave the arena, when Brynna shouted and Sam turned.

"There you are! Is that her?" Brynna pointed.

Sam nodded furiously, but the child had her around the neck now, and she could hardly talk.

"Yes," she croaked.

The riders came galloping out and Sam dodged behind Brynna. If Karla Starr saw her, it would be a warning.

When the riders were all through, the gates slammed closed.

"And now, folks, a little change in your program. The Cimmaron County rodeo is pleased to have Miss Karla Starr, former Best of the West rodeo queen and current president of Starr Rodeo Productions, as contractor for our little show. Miss Starr is proud of her stock, and because of some unfortunate publicity about her stallion, Renegade—"

"He's here!" Sam gasped.

Brynna was already shouting into her radio, trying to be heard over the noise all around.

"—directly across the arena, you'll see our cowboys all lined up. Give 'em a hand, folks, and watch the gate swing open for our rough-and-tumble, best-ever, wild horse race!"

Chapter Nineteen ⌒

$\mathcal{H}$ead high, muscles pumping, the Phantom exploded into the arena. The silver stallion claimed the attention of every person sitting in the stands.

At once, the crowd recognized the difference between a bucking horse and a wild mustang. He fled the dark, skyless place in which he'd been kept, following the wall of the arena as he would the high cliffs of home.

His desire to escape hardened every line of his body, making him beautiful despite his matted mane and dirt-smeared coat.

But he was muzzled.

Sam's head snapped back. They'd muzzled the great stallion like a dog.

It seemed she'd watched him for only a minute, while the world spun around her in a blur of color and music, but two of the teams had saddled their bucking horses and crossed the finish line. The others had given up.

One man in a blue shirt threw his hat in the dirt as the Phantom rounded the arena again. The stallion shied from the hat and ran toward a weak barrier where a calf-roping horse stood waiting. It must have looked like an opening, but it wasn't.

As the Phantom slowed, the man in blue saw his chance and grabbed the rope trailing from the stallion's muzzled head. Another man joined him, and then there were three, hanging on to the rope in a tug-of-war as the stallion bucked.

It was unfair, until the Phantom charged.

Dropping the rope, the men scattered with the stallion in pursuit. Others reached hands down for the men to grab. All but one man were pulled over the fence to safety.

A neigh floated across the arena, and the voice of that bucking horse made the Phantom swerve.

Was it an offer of help? Sam didn't know, but the stallion answered by galloping in that direction, even when he could see no way out. As his broad chest slammed into the chute, Sam felt it in her own heart.

Enough. She had to help him.

"Here." Suddenly aware of the child she was still holding, Sam shoved Darrell's cousin at Brynna.

"Sam, you're not—"

Some instinct made Brynna drop her radio to keep the child from falling. Relieved, Sam loosened her grip and escaped before Brynna could stop her.

She ran. Past all the closed arena gates, past the

faces of people she squirmed between. Sam ran until she could duck under a metal fence, into a maze of rails.

Brynna wouldn't follow her down this channel to the bucking chutes, because she wouldn't know where it led. These were just like the chutes she and Dallas had inspected at the Riverton and Sweetwater rodeos, only these were empty.

Sam heard the thunder of the Phantom's hooves. She was getting closer. She had to get into the arena before he hurt someone. What if he'd already trampled the man on the ground?

The smell of animals and manure told her she was getting closer. And still no one had followed.

All at once, Sam saw why.

A Brahma bull filled the space between the fences so completely, he couldn't turn. But he knew she was there. He bucked up, looking over the hump of flesh on his back to fix Sam with a glare.

"Maniac!" Sam gasped, transfixed by the mask of black and orange stripes on the bull's face.

She didn't have time to think what it meant, that Linc Slocum's bull was here. So was Karla Starr. And the Phantom. It all fit together somehow.

Maniac uttered a rumbling protest. Did he think she was attacking him from behind? Whatever the massive bull thought, he was furious. He loomed over her, coming fast as a truck in reverse, intent on running her down.

"It's okay, boy," Sam shouted. "It's okay."

Conversation wasn't going to work. He had no reason to think a human meant him well, she guessed, so Sam jumped for her way out.

Her fingers locked on a metal fence rail, then she pulled herself up, hand over hand, tennis shoes searching for each foothold. Maniac backed past her. She knew by the warm blast of breath and the splatter of moisture on the back of her favorite red blouse.

Over the top. Sam sprinted across the next narrow chute, over one more fence, and slid down the wall into the arena.

The Phantom saw her at once. The nervous pacing that had taken him around and around the arena stopped. He was still for only a minute, and then he rushed across the arena.

Sam heard gasps from the grandstands, and shouts summoning help, but she watched her horse. He galloped, head swinging from side to side, then lowered in a snaking, herding motion.

The Phantom stopped about six feet from her, and though every proud line of his body told Sam it was him, something was wrong. The stallion's head cocked to one side, then raised, eyes rolling, as if he couldn't see her clearly. Every sign of horse language she'd learned to read was scrambled.

More commotion rustled through the grandstands as the stallion arched his neck and pranced a circle around her. Some people caught their breath with awe. A few even clapped, thinking this was a performance.

In a way it was, but Sam turned, always facing the stallion, because she knew what came next. She'd seen this ritual both times the Phantom had fought Hammer.

There. A front leg struck out in challenge, and then he charged. Sam didn't close her eyes. He passed within inches, head swinging out as if to bite, and the metal muzzle struck Sam's shoulder. She felt impact, no pain, and a fierce stab of shame that the stallion might have bitten her if he could have.

The Phantom ran past, and from the corner of her eye, Sam saw a pickup man on a big dun horse, poised to help. Sam swallowed hard.

The Phantom pivoted and walked back. He looked more calm and he talked to her in a low, rumbling nicker, but his eyes still rolled, showing white around the brown.

Sam's world shrank to just this moment, just this horse. Everything depended on her skill at understanding him.

The stallion's forelegs braced apart and his head hung, mane falling forward, forelock covering his eyes. Sam made a quiet smooching and he staggered forward a step.

Inside the metal muzzle, the stallion's velvety lips moved. He lifted his head as if he might have nuzzled her if he could.

"Zanzibar, boy, what have they done to you?"

Grandstand sounds covered her voice, but the

stallion's ears pricked forward. He heard her. He knew her. He tried to come to her, but he had taken only two steps when he fell to his knees.

Unafraid, Sam ran to him. She ignored the rope trailing from his halter. Instead, she placed a hand on his withers.

"My poor boy," Sam murmured. The stallion's skin shivered at her touch, and he lurched up again.

With careful movements, Sam reached over the stallion's crest and lifted the halter over his ears. As it fell off his nose, the mustang shuddered. Sam wanted to grab the awful thing and throw it as far as her strength would let her. But that would shatter the Phantom's calm, so she just stroked him silently.

Through her dismay, Sam heard Brynna's voice.

"Sam, over here."

A gate swung open on oiled hinges, revealing a small pen. Seeing a way out, the stallion made for it.

The arena was silent as the stallion swayed step by step. Twice, he fell to his knees. Both times, Sam stood with her hand on his mane, talking, encouraging.

When the Phantom reached the enclosure and the gate closed behind him, his head flew up. A low cry said he recognized this final trap. In despair, he fell to his knees, to his side, and lay still.

Brynna grabbed Sam before she could get in the way of the team of vets who stood waiting. They swooped down upon the gray stallion, rolling back an eyelid, hydrating, monitoring his pulse and heartbeat.

Sam didn't know how long she watched before Brynna tried to explain.

"Drugs," Brynna said as she turned Sam to face her. "Karla Starr uses drugs to sedate her stock and to make them perform. She gave the Phantom something she calls Mad Dust. She cups it in her palms and blows it toward their nostrils."

Sam closed her eyes against an image of the copper-haired woman working black magic on the mustang.

"She claims it's legal. She also claims Slocum told her the stallion was his, and if she could catch him, she could have him—if she made Maniac a champion."

"He's here," Sam whispered, but she was watching the Phantom's legs twitch.

One of the vets spoke soothingly, though the stallion was unconscious. The vet's kindness made tears start up in Sam's eyes.

"We've impounded Maniac." Brynna's professional tone fell away for just a moment. "Tell me I didn't see right, that you weren't actually in the same chute with him, Samantha?"

Sam shook her head and Brynna sighed.

"Never mind. The important thing is, you're all right, and Karla Starr will have a lot to answer for in court, and the Bureau will pursue this case. I know it."

But that wasn't the important thing to Sam. She

put her hand out to still Brynna as the Phantom's legs churned more vigorously.

The kind vet she'd noticed before rose from his place beside the horse and came toward them. He was young and blond, with black-rimmed glasses, and his expression was full of hope.

"So far, so good," he said. "It's a blessing, really, that he's out, so we can work on him without causing further stress."

"Will he—" Sam couldn't ask the questions tumbling through her mind.

"His respiration is fine and his reflexes, though delayed, are improving. My name's Glen Scott, by the way."

He shook hands with Sam and Brynna, then glanced at the stocky woman who still sat by the horse while she talked on a cell phone. Just then, she gave him a thumbs-up.

"We've got a horse ambulance on the way, and if the stallion keeps improving, we'd recommend releasing him back to his environment as soon as possible."

"Dr. Scott"—Brynna's tone was hesitant—"don't you think he should be kept someplace overnight, for observation?"

Glen Scott shook his head and pushed his black glasses up his nose. Sam almost smiled, because he reminded her of Jen.

"That would mean more captivity and even more drugs." He looked earnest and determined to convince

Brynna. "Get another opinion if you like. But after what he's been through . . ." The vet shook his head.

"What about a week or two at the holding pens in Willow Springs? That would be safer," Brynna suggested.

"The life of a wild animal is never safe." Dr. Scott scanned the nearby pens, seeming to weigh the lives of the captive animals around them. "I think it will do more harm than good to keep him locked up. Why not drive all night, let him wake close to home, and release him?"

Home. Sam could picture the stallion, suddenly freed and galloping on the range where he belonged. The Phantom would face a challenger in his valley, though, and New Moon was young and strong.

Brynna turned to Sam. "It's your call, honey. What do you want for him?"

Safety or freedom. It should have been a simple choice. Safety meant the stallion's life would be filled with longing. Freedom might mean Sam had lost him forever.

She moved away from Brynna and crouched beside the Phantom. She'd never seem him down like this. It frightened her. She lay a hand on his neck. Beneath the sweat-stiff hair, his tiny blood vessels pulsed.

She'd heard of people who'd faced a firing squad and not been shot. Some never lost the fear they'd felt when they'd believed death was certain. Would the

Phantom be the same? Would he have the strength to drive New Moon away when the young horse had already served as king?

The Phantom's head lifted. His eyelids fluttered and then he lay still again.

"Bad dreams," the vet said. "His vital signs are improving all the time. Don't worry."

The Phantom trusted her. Terrified and filled with drugs, he'd come to her, allowed her to lead him from the arena by a piece of mane and the gentle pressure of her hand.

"Let's take him home," Sam said.

She leaned down and pressed her lips to his silver neck. It was a good-bye kiss. The Phantom would be safest if she never touched him again.

One mile past War Drum Flats, the sun rose and the desert turned tawny orange.

They'd driven all night. With the light, Sam saw frost edging the sagebrush at the roadside. It was cold out there and warm in the cab of Brynna's truck, but Sam shoved the door open and ran to the horse ambulance the minute the vehicle braked to a stop.

Hooves pounded inside, and the Phantom screamed. Sounds that would have horrified her two weeks ago made Sam glad. He was awake and strong and ready to be free.

Dr. Scott met Sam behind the vehicle. The stallion's neigh vibrated the ambulance. His kicks rocked it.

The vet rubbed his hands together and blew on them. Cold, but heartened by the mustang's vigor, he smiled as he surveyed the high desert landscape.

"It's gorgeous out here," he said. "And I think this mustang smells home."

Sam nodded and followed the vet's glance as he watched Brynna stride nearer.

"Last chance to take him up to Willow Springs," Brynna told Sam. "We could keep him there until we've removed the black from the herd. Kind of ease the transition."

Staring at the dark road, their headlights the only light for miles, they'd talked about this for hours last night, and Sam's answer never changed.

"No." She shook her head. That would mean revealing the Phantom's hideaway. Never again would his mares and foals be safe. "It's time."

Metal bolts clanged. Hinges squeaked.

The stallion backed out, kicking. Brynna, Sam, and the vet stepped away, but not far enough. The Phantom's head snaked toward the humans, scattering them farther off.

Sam didn't speak. She didn't try to soothe him. That part of their friendship was over.

The great silver stallion swung to face the mountains. He took a single breath, loosed a mighty neigh, and launched himself away. In seconds, only a white spiral of dust nearly a mile away suggested that a mustang traveled a narrow zigzag trail.

The stallion didn't look back and Sam didn't cry.

She didn't reply when Brynna spoke to her, either, or join in her thanks to Dr. Scott, although she wanted to.

Instead, she stared at the ground, where a faint sifting of sand had caught the Phantom's running hoofprints. Shallow and far apart, they held morning light and tiny shadows. She walked the path he had taken until the ground hardened and she lost her way.

Behind her, Sam heard Brynna tell Dr. Scott the BLM would be in touch regarding the cost of doctoring the mustang. She should go back, but she wanted to hang on to the Phantom for just a few minutes more.

Sam heard a screech and looked up. She squinted, letting her eyelashes filter the brightness enough that she could watch the red-tailed hawk wheel in a dark silhouette against the morning sun.

A messenger to the sky spirits. That's what Jake had told her just before the flash flood struck. She hadn't wished then, but now she did.

"I don't want him to be gone forever," Sam whispered. "I just want to see him. I love his wildness. I'll never try to take it away."

Sam closed her dazzled eyes. A frenzy of multicolored lights from staring at the sun made her dizzy. When she opened her lids, the hawk was gone.

Sam trudged back toward Brynna's truck. The horse ambulance was bouncing away, leaving twin wisps of dust behind. Brynna must be waiting in her truck.

There was no sense putting it off. It was time for her to go home, too. Sam hurried, then hesitated. She detoured just a little to her right, to see what lay on the ground.

Was the sun still playing tricks with her vision? Sam refused to believe her eyes until she stood right over it. Between her dirty tennis shoes lay a feather. It glinted red-brown and glossy against the white desert floor.

She smiled and bent to pick it up. Between thumb and forefinger, she held the feather's spine, then smoothed her fingers along the perfect plume.

The red-tailed hawk had given her a sign.

Sam's wish for the silver stallion had been heard.

From
Phantom Stallion
⚬∾ 5 ⚬∾
FREE AGAIN

Sam CLIMBED OUT of Gram's Buick and slammed the door harder than necessary. She crossed her arms and stared across the parking area at the corrals of captive mustangs.

She wanted to ignore Brynna Olson's cheery arrival, but the woman's freckled face actually brightened when she saw them.

"Sam, Grace, good to see you."

Gram gave Brynna a quick hug, and Sam's spirits sank lower. *A hug*. Things were worse than she thought, but at least Brynna didn't try it with her. Just in case, Sam took a step back.

Brynna's smile vanished. Her face clouded with confusion.

"Sam"—Brynna's tone turned clipped and formal—"I want you to look at some horses for me."

"The unadoptables. Gram told me. Will they be destroyed?"

"BLM doesn't destroy healthy horses," Brynna said. "But I'm worried about this bunch."

The wind kicked up a whirlwind of dust. Brynna detoured around it. So did Gram and Sam.

Brynna stopped outside a corral shaded by a wall of stacked hay bales. About a dozen horses stood inside the pen.

Gram took an audible breath and let it go. "They're not much to look at. I can't say I'd pay good money for any of them."

Sam leaned against the corral fence and studied the horses a minute longer. She hated to admit it, but most people would agree with Gram.

The horses didn't look like mustangs. Glossy and well-fed, maybe too well-fed, they looked bored and undisturbed by the humans at the fence.

The group was made up of one black, three paints, and assorted bays and sorrels.

"The most outstanding things about them are their ages and lousy conformation," Brynna said.

Sam didn't want to agree, but Brynna was right.

One bay mare had a ewe neck that looked too weak to support her head. A tall bay's showy white socks only emphasized his sickle-hocked hind legs. The black's ears stayed pinned against his neck as if he were permanently cranky, and the scars on his hind legs said he'd kicked—or been kicked—plenty. The smallest of the paints had bumps from withers to tail, as if he'd been stung by a hive of bees. The largest of the paints had a huge belly, leaving no doubt about who got to the feed first.

Sam tried to pick one horse she'd want for her own. It wasn't easy.

The liver chestnut looked pretty good. He strutted like a stallion, and the other horses gave him room, but his extreme Roman nose gave him the face of a fierce dinosaur.

Wait. Sam moved a little farther down the fence. What about that sorrel? Ears pricked and eyes wide, she was a pretty little animal whose flaxen mane streamed over her cinnamon shoulders like honey.

"She's beautiful," Sam said. "I can't believe no one would adopt her."

As Sam pointed her out, the filly trotted toward the fence.

All at once, Sam ached with pity. The filly's knees were aimed to the sides instead of straight ahead. Her gait was so wobbly, Sam feared she'd fall.

"She's young," Brynna said. "Those legs might straighten out, or they could be corrected by surgery. She is a beauty. Plus, she's curious and eager to learn." Brynna paused and shook her head. "But no one's willing to take a chance on her."

"Did they all come from around here?" Gram asked.

"No. They're from all over the place—Oregon, California, some from down near Las Vegas. Only one of the paints could be called local." Brynna gestured south. "The big one came in with a bunch from the Smoke Creek desert."

Though her voice was all business, Brynna wiggled her fingers toward the sorrel filly, tempting her a few steps closer. "These horses have been moved from one adoption center to another," she continued.

"And that's why they're so tame?" Sam interrupted.

Brynna nodded. "They've been loaded and unloaded, herded, and fed by humans. Some have been captive for over a year. When they leave here next week, they'll go to a big pasture in the Midwest where they'll stay for life."

"That doesn't sound so bad," Gram said. "Though I'm not sure I like the fact that my tax dollars will be supporting a retirement home for horses."

"Lots of folks feel that way," Brynna admitted.

As the two women discussed money, Sam wished she could turn these horses loose and watch them run free. They'd look like different animals. But they'd probably never gallop across the range again. These mustangs would graze away their lives, placid as dairy cows.

Sam turned around in time to see Brynna fall silent. Words seemed to jam in her throat as she glanced back toward her office. "I'm leaving for two weeks of meetings in Washington, D.C. Norman White is taking my place. He's"—Brynna seemed to be biting her tongue to stay professional—"not a horseman," she managed. "And I'm not sure what decisions might be made while I'm gone."

Sam watched Brynna shift, then swallow hard. Why was the woman so uneasy?

Sam sorted through all Brynna had said today, until her mind clicked on a single phrase.

BLM doesn't destroy healthy horses.

Was Brynna worried that Norman White wouldn't certify these mustangs as healthy?

But Brynna's and Gram's conversation had supplied the reason. Money.

Norman White might try to save the government money by having old or ill-formed horses put down.

Not only would that be cruel, it would be unfair. These horses were wild animals. They hadn't been bred to measure up to human standards.

"How can I help?" Sam asked.

"Do you know anyone who'd want them?" Brynna didn't sound very hopeful.

"That's it?" Sam asked. Surely, Brynna could come up with something better than that. "Didn't you ask me up here to help with some plan?"

Brynna shook her head, looking forlorn. "I've run out of plans and time," she said.

Sam did her best to consider the horses all over again.

If she were a millionaire, she'd adopt them, put them in a huge pasture, and hope their wild natures returned. But she knew only one millionaire, and he'd never help. All Linc Slocum's possessions were beautiful or valuable. These horses were neither.

Who, then? Jake's Three Ponies Ranch couldn't afford twelve useless horses. Jen's family had already been forced to sell their land and stock to Slocum. Sam couldn't think of anyone with both a soft heart and money.

"What about the HARP program?" Sam said suddenly. "These horses would be perfect. The little sorrel is half tame already. And kids would like those pintos."

"I already tried HARP," Brynna said. "Their funding is looking shaky. They won't take on more horses or kids until it's a sure thing."

Sam stared at the captive mustangs until they blurred. Who would want a dozen horses, mostly old and ugly?

Sam rubbed her eyes. "Dust from that whirlwind," she muttered to Gram and Brynna. But Sam was thinking, *They don't deserve to die.*